The First Angel
Copyright @ 2017 by Thomas R. Brown
ISBN 978-13-7059972-1

First Edition: March 2017

I0620666

ACKNOWLEDGMENTS

This book is a ten year effort with a lot of tears and doubts.

It started as a simple bedtime story to my children. Encouraged by my wife and children, I started the venture of writing.

As many new writers will know, self-doubt is always pressing on your shoulders. Any self-imposed deadline becomes nebulous and fraught with the inevitable delays. Even when completed, countless rewrites and edits become the ever ending excuse to not to finish.

Fortified with my family's backing, I found the real cause of the telling of the First Angel.

Many of us have seen horror movies or read a book where the devil, often times disguised as a malevolent being, is the central character that plays on our every fear. As a fan of horror, as I watch these demon laden movies, I often ask the question: truly, if there is a devil, then there must be an angel. But, rarely, if ever, do you see an angel in these movies.

As I often ask my children after watching a horror flick, "Why can't the main character call on an angel like he/she did with the devil?"

The First Angel does that. It counterbalances

the evil there is in this universe with the good that I think God intended.

Hope you enjoy this book. Remember, angels are all around us. All you have to do is look.

***

This book is dedicated to my mother whom I hope to see in heaven someday.

Also, to my wife, Sora, the person that I love and hope to be together forever.

"And now war broke out in heaven, when Michael with his angels attacked the dragon. The dragon fought back with his angels, but they were defeated and driven out of heaven."   Revelations 12:7-8

Archangel Hierarchy (Note: One Legion = 5,004 angels)

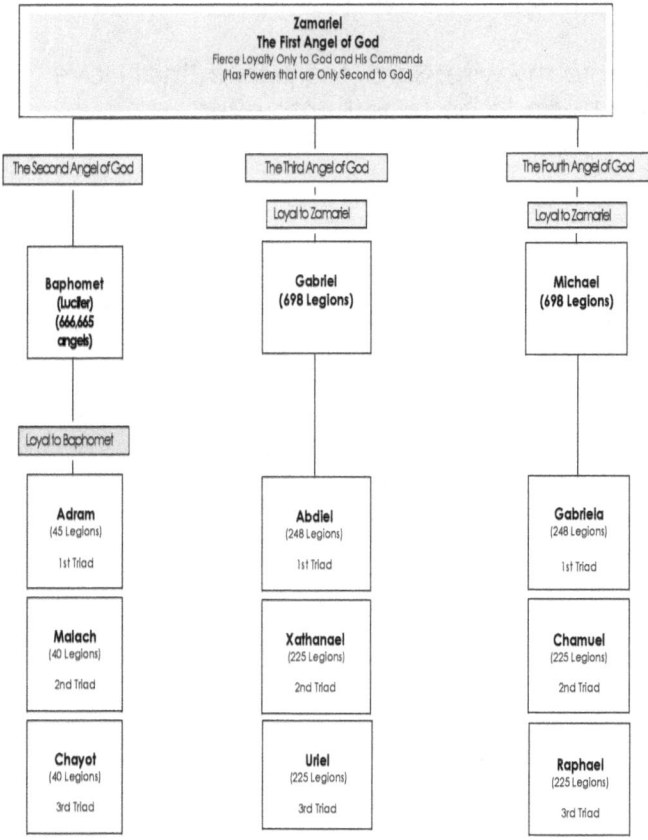

"In the beginning God created heaven and earth."
Genesis 1:1

Introduction:

Nineteen to the Nineteenth power millennium
years ago, before there was a universe, before there
was a single molecule, before there was Adam, and
after God became lonely, God created the angels to
keep his company.

Colossians 1:16-7

*"For by Him all things were created, both in the heavens
and on earth, visible and invisible, whether thrones or
dominions or rulers or authorities – all things have been
created by Him and for Him. And He is before all things,
and in Him all things hold together."*

God did not create angels as glorified human
beings. They are not capable of marriage or
reproduce like humans. However, like humans,
they have free will and can fall in love.

God made 7,777,777 angels and no new angels are
being added to that number.

Since they are angels, they are not killed in the
human sense, but destroyed. After they are
destroyed, there is no heaven or hell for them to go;
they become non-existent, as God had intended.
Angels cannot be destroyed by any other of God's
creations except by God and by other angels.
Angels can manifest themselves in various living

forms like spirits or as "ghosts" or as an animal or come in any living form.

God named his first Angel, Zamariel. Zamariel is extremely loyal to God and he is as powerful as he is kind. Other angels have abundant love for Zamariel second only to God. For all this, God loves him the most.

And for all of this, a rift in heaven was created. For the second angel that God created was named Lucifer.

"Blessed are the meek for they will inherit the land."   Matthew 5:5

Prelude Being Human

"Stay down, wimp!"

Aslin could taste the blood in his mouth. As long as he could remember, kids from school always bullied him. And as always, he never fought back because of the promise he made to his mother.

A promise he made when he was in kindergarten and has never broken since.

It was the fourth day of school of Aslin's third grade. It was a chilly 28 degrees Fahrenheit and clear blue skies. For the third time in as many days, three sixth grade boys that walked from the same neighborhood from home to school and back, did their usual.

"Hey look! It's Aslin, the ass-wipe," laughed Mark, the meanest boy of the bunch.

He was the tallest and had the meanest pair of eyes that reminded Aslin of a rat. Mark's teasing was always followed by a gut punch with a succession of smacks to the back of the head.

Tears started flowing from Aslin's eyes as he could not decide what hurt more, his stomach or the back of his head that made him see stars.

"Woo hoo, the little ass-wipe is crying like a baby,"

taunted Jimmy who's brown circler freckles dotted his face that was framed by a shock of red hair that was gelled up to a spike.

Not to be left out, Connor, the chubby one of the bunch, pushed him from behind that made Aslin fall on his chest that knocked the breath out of him.

As he panted, slowly rising to his feet, Aslin choked on his tears, "Please leave me alone!"

"Or what? What are you going to do about it, ass-wipe?" Mark stood over Aslin and stared down on him with his rat eyes. "That's what I thought, nothing! You loser!"

The three walked away laughing with satisfaction. Aslin started to walk as best as he can in the other direction and at the same time wiping away his tears and runny nose with the sleeve of his right arm.

"Hey, ass-wipe, we'll see you tomorrow. If you don't want to get your ass stomped again, bring us ten dollars. If you don't, we'll come over and take it out on your sweet little mother," sneered Mark.

Here those words coming out of Mark's mouth, Aslin stopped in his tracks and turned toward the three boys and calmly and in almost in a whisper said haltingly, "What did you say about my mother?"

Puzzled that this small insignificant boy would even address them, Mark turned towards Aslin and walked towards him trailed by the other two boys.

"What? Did you say something ass-wipe?"

Again in a barely audible voice, Aslin asked again, "What did you say about my mother?"

Mark looked at his two chums and started to laugh uncontrollably as the other two followers joined in with their own chorus of boyish howling.

"I said that your mother will be begging for my..." before all of the words could come out of Mark's mouth, Aslin bull rushed him.

Mark was about a foot taller than Aslin, so Aslin jumped to the height where his head was a foot above Mark's. At his phoenix, Aslin's small, yet powerful right fist came crashing down like an anvil on Mark's nose instantly breaking it as evidenced by a crunching sound and smatter of blood on Mark's face like a bucket of red paint thrown on an empty canvas.

Mark's beady eyes rolled back in his head that was replaced by the white of his eyes that bulged through his eye sockets. He fell backwards unconsciously knocking both Connor and Jimmy on their butts.

Aslin landed on his feet in a crouch ready for another attack. A small boy of eight now looked like a tiny but a fierce and a fearsome warrior.

Whether it was the blow that they witnessed or

because of Aslin's scary posture of attack, both Jimmy and Connor blurted out, "OK, OK, stop, we're sorry."

Jimmy pushed himself from under Mark's body.

"Oh my God! We need to get help. I think Mark is really hurt."

Mark still lay unconscious. By then, a man and a woman passing by who witnessed the tail end of the fierce blow inflicted by Aslin, after recovering from their astonishment, rushed over to the group. The woman knelt next to Mark and cradled his head while the man standing next to them fished out his cell phone from his coat pocket.

"Hello, yes, we need an ambulance..."

Fast forward 10 years later and he is still getting bullied. Ever since the third grade fiasco that put Mark in a coma for two weeks, after numerous police inquiries, threats of prison for delinquents, and lawsuits from Mark's parents, Aslin stopped fighting.

His promise not to fight anymore did not so much come from what happened on that fateful day when he was eight, but how he felt about what he done. First, he could not believe the uncontrollable rage he felt and the power he possessed. He knew, even at age eight, he had some sort of power that made him scared and curious. His mother and father told him that he was special, but warned him that he must never use his strength for any reason whatsoever. People would not understand.

The truth be known, Aslin did not understand it either, but a promise was a promise. Besides, he could never live with himself if he ever hurt someone again. Mark's almost death experience gave Aslin nightmares and only after he turned 16, did the nightmares became less frequent and only because it was replaced by another.

"For it is written: He will command his angels concerning you to guard you carefully…"   *Luke 4:10*

Chapter 1 the First Encounter

"I am from God," she said.

It all started about a week ago.

It was around 11 at night, raining sideways from the angry winds from the north, and the bone chilling cold it carried with it.

Aslin was coming home from the Issaquah Highlands after watching a movie that he wished he didn't go see. He often went to the movies by himself. He felt like a loser because he didn't quite feel like he connected with anyone. He had very few friends over the years because any beginnings of a friendship always ended up wrong.

He pulled into the concrete driveway with his old fire red '65 Ford Mustang with six inch rear lifts that made the car look like a small red dragon on steroids. He really loved his car.

Every day Aslin would wax the car so much that he was waxing the wax until you could see his face in the paint like a mirror. The four cylinder motor burned oil that scorched a hole in his wallet trying to keep up with the massive supply of oil that he had to feed the car every week to keep it running. This was his most treasured baby. He loved his first car. It was a gift from his parents.

Through the screechy windshield wipers that hardly did its job, Aslin strained his eyes through the foggy tainted windshield and windswept rain, to see her for the first time, standing at the end of the small concrete driveway, tall, lanky, and beautiful. She was elegant and took the breath out of him as he swerved yanking his wheel to the left trying to avoid driving on the grass as he made up the driveway.

The lone figure staring up into the wet sky, as the rain plastered strands of her blonde hair against her lily-white face, Aslin as closer he got, felt a familiarity. Her face was so white that it seemed like it was glowing, even at a night like this. The rain was pelting her green almond shaped eyes, but she wasn't blinking.

Aslin couldn't take his eyes off of her as he opened the door of his car. As usual, the door creaked loud enough to hear a block away even cutting through the noise of the rain and the wind. As Aslin climbed out of the car, he was immediately pelted by bullet sized raindrops immediately smacked by a heavy arm of wind that banged the door shut.

His brown hair had no chance to lie quietly on his head as the restless storm tossed it in wild directions. The car sounds and the near hurricane weather didn't seem like it had any effect on this lonely figure of a girl as she continued to look towards the stormy gray sky.

Aslin slowly walked the four paces to her as the

rain shelled his face. The rain and the wind was so hard he had to strain his eyes open lest he got water and debris in them. Amidst this natural chaos, in her bare footed calmness, she was wearing a white flowing gown that stuck to her well-formed body that showed every curve and bump. Even with the mean spirited weather swirling around them, Aslin felt a strange calmness coming from this strange and beautiful female standing there with such grace and poise.

As Aslin got closer to her, he shouted through the storm, "Are you OK?"

She didn't move a muscle and kept staring up in the sky. Aslin got closer; close enough to almost touch her.

A lightning lit the sky followed with a loud clap of thunder that made Aslin jump and Aslin knew that the storm was right on top of them. Even then, this beautiful girl in front of him was oblivious to the turmoil around her.

"Hey, are you OK, can I help you?" Aslin shouted again.

She lowered her head towards him and blinked. It seemed that her green eyes pierced right through him. Her pupils were blue as a clear sky surrounded by amazingly bright green irises and the whites of her eyes were the color of bright egg whites. It sent shivers down his back. She parted her ample lips as water was dripping down simultaneously from the tip of her nose and from the point of her beautiful narrow chin and said nothing. A three seconds later that seemed so much longer, she went back to staring into the angry sky.

She was about 5 foot 7 inches, so Aslin was looking at her at a downward angle when he noticed a fleeting smile cross her soft red lips like she knew something so secret that only she knew and wanted to tell someone, but held back the temptation to do so.

"You want to come in out from the rain?" Aslin anxiously asked again, but this time in an almost in a whisper that she couldn't possibly have heard through the gale.

Without any pause, to his surprise, she turned and started for the front door.

Chapter 2 Help Needed

Aslin fumbled with his keys as she waited for him to find the keyhole.

Aslin opened the front door with the same key more times than he can count and on any given day probably can open it with his eyes closed, but tonight, he can't seem to find the right key or the keyhole. Aslin quickly noticed that while she stood next to him, he could feel the warmth of her body and hear the whisper of her breathing. It made him fumble more with the door. Finally, Aslin found the bulls-eye, Aslin got the door opened and swung it wide for her to enter.

She just stood there. As Aslin took the full breadth of her being not more than six inches from him, he suddenly noticed a sweet fragrance coming from her. It was a mixture of lavender and chamomile and it was intoxicating.

"Ah, you want to come in?" Aslin said haltingly.

She blinked and then walked into his house and into his life.

"I'll get us some towels so that we can dry off," Aslin said.

While Aslin turned, as she was standing in the foyer, he nearly tripped over his own two feet as he headed towards the half bathroom off the living room. His home, a two bedroom and one and a half bathroom house, is one of two possessions left to him by his parents. He is proud of his little house and keeps it clean and orderly.

This house brings back memories. Aslin was born here, had his first birthday here, had his first kiss on the blue living room sofa, and for the past two years, mourned here alone.

It was also in this house, Aslin felt the most secure and happy. His parents always made him feel special when he didn't feel like he was. It is here that Aslin first learned the lessons of life, its pleasures and its losses.

Once, when Aslin was nine years old, on a cool summer Friday around 8 o'clock in the evening, he heard a loud skidding sound in front of their house followed by a thud like a car hitting something soft.

Aslin immediately went out to see what happened. That's when he saw a car pulling away leaving a mound of golden hair lying in the middle of the road.

As Aslin approached closer, he quickly realized that it was their neighbor's dog, a Golden Labrador. Golden Labs are known for their friendly and loyal disposition always wagging their tail in greeting at someone that they knew.

The neighbors would sometimes allow Aslin to walk him and play stick. As he knelt down over his body, the only thing the dog could do is whimper in pain. He must have gotten out of his outdoor pen after his owners left for the weekend to visit their in-laws two states over, Aslin thought. He started to wheeze in pain and looked up with his moist eyes as if imploring Aslin to stop the pain. It broke Aslin's heart.

Aslin picked him up and brought him to the house. He laid him softly on the living room couch. His dad examined him as gently as possible. The dog had his left front and both of his rear legs broken and probably has several broken ribs, but they couldn't really tell. He had blood coming out of his mouth and his nostrils.

Aslin begged his dad to take him to the vet, but the nearest vet was about 70 miles away and besides, it didn't look like he was going to survive much longer. Aslin could tell he was in great pain, but they didn't have anything to ease his pain or to put him down.

Aslin sat with him and told him, "It will be OK."

Aslin knew he was lying. Aslin prayed with all the conviction he could muster and he implored God to save him.

At 11:25 that night, Aslin was suddenly awaken from a dozing sleep as the dog rolled his big Labrador head and looked at him and gave a final low yelp before his head rolled on the pillow and took his last breath.

Aslin wept. His name was Gabriel.

When Aslin got back to the foyer, she wasn't there.

He went searching in the living room, "Hello, I have the towels."

She wasn't there either. He half ran to the kitchen, back to the bathroom, and then back to the living room.

Aslin is 6 foot and 1 inch on a good shadowy day and weighs about 180 pounds after eating about five juicy cheeseburgers with a large chocolate milkshake, two of them, of course. He always had a big appetite. Girls use to tease him that he had gigantic hands and feet and he should try out for the wrestling team and wear those tight wrestling singlets. Aslin was not sure what big hands had to do with wrestling, but girls always been a mystery to him.

Aslin was an "A" student, but since his parent's always discouraged him from playing sports, he took up the piano. It was easy for him to learn and since his mom was the teacher, Aslin received as many lessons as he could tolerate.

So, it's no surprise that people see him as a tall lanky piano playing nerd, and hence, he often goes to the movies by himself. Needless to say, Aslin is no lady's man. Every time a girl comes up to him, his tongue gets twisted into knots and it seems like this is happening more often than not. Just going to the movies is tough especially when the ticket person is a girl. It seems a day doesn't go by when a girl that Aslin doesn't even know walks up to him and starts talking to him about the weather or something. A puzzling behavior, Aslin thought.

In eighth grade, Aslin had a friend that happened to be a girl who came closest to being a girlfriend that Aslin ever had. She was great. Her name was Uriel.

She was beautiful, smart, and funny. They did everything together. They went to the movies, went to the eight grade dance, shared banana splits, and even one time, she let him touch her left breast. She said her left breast was bigger. Aslin couldn't really tell the difference by looking at them.

Their friendship didn't last very long. She suddenly moved about a year after Aslin became friends with her. Aslin didn't know why, but they never stayed in contact. He often wondered what happened to her. Even now, he feels a pang of loss and loneliness thinking about her.

His mom said that Aslin had character and inner strength that wasn't learned, but that he was born with it. She said some people have a gift to be a natural leader, where others, have natural disposition to follow. He, she said, was a natural born leader. Aslin wasn't sure if this was true or just another mother proudly talking about her only son. Aslin never had the desire to lead anyone nor led anyone to anything, let alone, feel like a leader of some sort.

"Oh no," Aslin whispered to himself, "I let a beautiful wacko into the house and she's probably going to kill me or something."

He was not in the habit of talking to himself, but it's not every day that a stranger walks into his life who happens to be a hot looking babe.

Hot or not, there is something about her. Aslin couldn't put his finger on it, but even when he was in a different room and had no clue as to where she was in the house, he felt strangely tranquil.

His logic said that only a crazy person would stand in the rain and enters a stranger's house. He was probably crazier for letting her in. But still, without an exchange of words or so much as a glance, Aslin felt connected to this person.

Finally, after few seconds that seem longer, Aslin got the nerve to shout halfheartedly, more out of trepidation then courage, "OK, you can come out now. I'm serious!"

Frustrated, Aslin walked back to his bedroom. He nearly jumped out of his twelve and a half loafers. There she was lying on his bed. As far as he could tell she was sleeping. She was beautiful.

You could see a slight rise and fall of her chest. That was not the only thing Aslin was staring at. As if she sensed his thoughts, she opened her eyes and lifted her hand towards him and gestured with her hands to come to her.

Aslin wanted to say something like, "Hey, what's up," something cool and nonchalant. But, his mouth wouldn't move; it was dry. He made a loud gulping sound as he swallowed the lump in his throat. His breathing became heavier as he approached her.

He was only about four short steps from her, but he felt like she was a mile away. The four seconds that took him to cross the blue worn out rug seemed like he was walking under water. He knew he was using the same walking mechanics that he normally used and he knew that he was actually getting to his destination, but it seemed like it was taking him minutes to get there instead of seconds.

Aslin finally arrived, still soaking wet. His hair was plastered down on his head like cement. His shirt was clinging to his chest, so you could see his well-built pecs through his shirt. He wiped the wetness from his brow and stood there transfixed on her lovely serene face. He could have stood there for eternity just staring.

She looked deeply into his brown eyes and spoke her first words to him, "Will you help me?"

"Sure," Aslin said slowly as he came out of his trance without thinking about the consequences of his answer, as he would later find out.

After quickly coming to his senses, Aslin said, "Wait, and help you with what?"

She rose from the queen size bed that used to be his parents.

Chapter 3 Mom and Dad

His parents died in a freaky car accident about two years ago when Aslin was 16 years old and two years from his high school graduation. He was their only child. Aslin thought of himself as a typical teenager, but with one major difference.

Aslin actually loved his parents and got along with them really well. He couldn't remember when he ever crossed words with his parents. Mind you, Aslin was no saint. One time, in the cafeteria, he took an extra desert without asking the cafeteria monitor. He was sweating bullets after that incident and vowed that he will never compromise his ethics again.

It was a good thing that his parents were the most understanding people on earth. His friends, the few that he had, but now gone, always teased him that they wished they had parents like his that let him do anything that he wanted. Maybe because of that freedom, Aslin never really wanted to do anything bad like stay out past curfew, or skip classes or some other teenage mischievousness.

His parents were the typical mid-western couple. His dad worked at the hardware store and his mom volunteered at the church. They belonged to a non-denominational church. They weren't rich, but weren't poor. His dad didn't drive a fancy car nor did his mom ever wanted any expensive dresses or make-up and such.

To Aslin looking back growing up with his parents, his memories were always of happiness in a contented family that was very average.

For almost two years, Aslin kept going over his head how his parents died. It was a chilly November night with slight hint of wind passing by now and then. They rarely went out without him, but that night, they went out on their first ever "date night" to see a movie. They were due home around 11 that night.

"Are you sure, you'll be OK?" His mom, the worrier, asked for the fifth time in the last 15 minutes.

"Yes, for the millionth time! What can go wrong? Don't worry about me, I am just going to read and probably watch some TV. Have fun! "Aslin said with slight exasperation.

They said their goodbyes; little did Aslin know that it was to be their last.

Through weeks of grieving, there was always something that kept nagging Aslin about their deaths. First of all, why that particular night did they go out, especially when they never went out alone without him? Never.

Aslin was old enough to know that married couples once in a while needed "alone" time together away from their kids and take a break, but the desire to go out that night was sudden. The police report said that their car went under a trailer of an 18-wheeler semi-truck and both were decapitated. The image gave him nightmares for months.

Aslin checked the weather of the night of the accident from different weather reporting sources. It was chilly that night, but not freezing. The temperature ranged from 38 to 42 degrees Fahrenheit, so the car accident couldn't be blamed on frozen roads.

Aslin tracked down the trucker who happened to live one town over. His name was John Carlson. He lived in an old apartment building at the edge of town where people would refer to it as the "dump". Aslin went to see him to find out what actually happened.

When Aslin knocked on door of the second floor unit, Aslin heard a gruff voice, "Who is it!"

"It's Aslin Benie, the son of Michael and Gabriela. I want to talk to you about the accident," Aslin replied while staring at the one-way peephole.

Few seconds later, Aslin heard some shuffling sound and another sound that sounded like a whimpering dog, so Aslin finally said, "Can I speak with you just for a few minutes?"

Another few seconds passed in silence.

Without a word, the door opened. Standing there in blue bedroom slippers and a matching bathrobe that had its share of coffee stains, he beckoned

Aslin in. He silently led him down a short and dark hallway to the green walled kitchen.

There were pile of dishes in the sink, trash littered on the floor, and empty vodka bottles scattered throughout the kitchen. His breath reeked of alcohol and his body odor smelled like a dirty wet sock that needed to be thrown away because no amount of detergent could wash it.

"I don't know why you're here. I don't have any money, if that's what you are looking for. If you want revenge, go ahead and take your best shot," he half shouted with irritation from a person who seem to have nothing to lose since he already has lost it all, all the while looking down at the empty vodka bottles and licking his lips.

"I just came here to ask some questions about that night and then I will be on my way," Aslin replied.

John kept looking down at the floor and every few seconds his whole head would twitch sideways then few seconds later his whole head would gyrate up and down like one of those uncontrollable bobble heads on a car dashboard.

He was a wreck that already happened. He explained that he stopped driving a truck after the accident. He has nightmares every night.

Aslin asked him about his nightmares, not because he wanted to know, but because at that point in time, Aslin too was still having nightmares and was bit surprised that he was not the only one.

John's nightmares always started the same way, he explained. A man covered in shadows is standing in the middle of the road. His face is covered by darkness, so you couldn't make out his facial features. As he gets closer to this man, it becomes apparent that he is holding something in both of his hands.

Repeatedly, in these nightmares, the man slowly raises his left arm and shows a decapitated head.

The bodiless and pale face had the look of terror with the eyes wide opened with a focused attention of fear. The head was wrenched from the torso. Hanging from the bottom were various strands of spaghetti like veins dripping with blood.

It was the head of Aslin's father that mournfully shouts repeatedly, "The end of the beginning has begun!"

In the right hand, the shadowy man lifts the head of Aslin's mother.

She too has the same fear in her eyes, but her face shows contradictory expressions of serenity and peace as she laments repeatedly, "Wake up! We need you!"

Aslin was shaken by this man's dream. He whispered to John, "How do you know that the heads are my mother's and father's?"

He just nodded his head silently while he fingered his rosary beads hanging from his neck that Aslin didn't first notice at the door.

Finally, John looked up and said, "Because the thing holding the heads told me."

John started crying uncontrollably.

And then he said the strangest thing that was not in the police report, "There was someone standing in the middle of road that night, that's when I lost control of my truck. I swear, after my truck jack knifed, my trailer skidded sideways almost close enough for me to touch out of my driver side window, I got out of the truck to see if I hit someone, but there was nobody around."

After Aslin told him that the police report made no mention of how he lost control, he looked at Aslin with tears streaming down his unshaven face and swore again that he swerved to miss someone that night that was standing in the middle of the road.

There were no witnesses, so Aslin didn't know if John was hallucinating or if there was really a person in his path.

"I am so sorry about your mom and dad," he said chokingly. Aslin felt sorry for him, too.

Seven days later, his daughter called Aslin to tell him that her father passed away. He died of a heart attack four days after Aslin visited him.

When Aslin asked her what made her call him, she said that her father scrawled a message that was found next to his body the day he passed away. The police said they only knew of one person with the same name that her father referred to in his message that was connected to him.

The note said: "Beware Aslin, they are coming for you."

Aslin had no idea what this meant. Who is coming for me and why? Was this connected to the death of his parents or to John's nightmares?

With the help of a sympathetic friend, who is a whiz at hacking, Aslin was able to get hold of his parents' coroner's reports. He found a very strange twist to this already horrifying drama unfolding in his life.

His parents' necks were sliced cleanly at the precisely at the same location on their respective necks. It was as if a scalpel followed a precise line that was drawn on their necks. The coroner's report attributed the cuts to the flying glass broken from the windshield.

After months of obsession with his parents' death that was adding to two years, Aslin gave up. He gave up on that rainy night when he met the girl with the blue green almond shaped eyes.

Chapter 4 Zamariel

"Help me prepare for your destiny as God's greatest angel." She said those words with calm and conviction that Aslin almost believed her.

It was at that moment that he noticed that she was completely dry. Her white gown had no signs of moisture. Her hair was salon perfect, long and wavy that flowed on each side of her head and down to her shoulders. And then, it struck him like a lightning bolt of the meaning of her words. He knew for sure that she was a wacko. Beautiful or not, he was going to get her out of his house. Now!

As if she was able to read his mind and before, he could say anything, she said, "I know, Zamariel, you are confused".

Confused? You got that right lady, he thought.

"First of all, my name is not Zamariel. It's…"

Before Aslin could say his human name, she said, "Aslin, meaning the 'The One'".

"How did you know my name?" Aslin asked and quickly realized that it was a stupid question because you can look up anyone's name on the Internet. All you have to do is Google it.

"Zamariel, please sit down and let me explain."

Aslin hesitantly sat next to her on the bed. Her

piercing blue green eyes were beautiful as much as they gave him the creeps.

When time didn't exist, she explained, God was here. Since time and location is a man-made invention, it will be hard to explain where God came from and where he is. God is not limited by time or space since its boundaries only governs what He has created.

At this point, Aslin didn't have a clue of what she was talking about and she sensed that. So, she explained to him, in order for him to understand, she will speak in earthly terms.

God has a great plan, a plan that has not been fulfilled yet. One can say that it's a work in progress. Before the universe was created, God made the angels. The angels, like it says in some earthly religions, were not made to be his messengers. There were made to protect the next stage of His plan, which was the creation of the universe and all its inhabitants.

He made 7,777,777 angels with different strengths and weaknesses. They have free will and extraordinary powers, second only to God. God made the first four angels as His special guardians of the plan. All the other angels were made to serve God and the four angels.

The four angels also had a hierarchy, a chain of command. The ranking of the angels were very simple. The rest of the angels ranked based on the order that they were created. Angels do not have a genders like humans, but can fall in love. They can come in many forms; as an animal, a human, or any other living creature. She referred to all of the angels as a "he" regardless of the gender that they transformed into when conducting God's bidding.

The first angel God created was Zamariel.

He was made as the leader and the most powerful angel. Zamariel became God's most trusted and loyal angel and because of this, many angels felt God favored him the most. Zamariel exceled in angel swordsmanship with lightning speed and craftiness. Over the millennium, he demonstrated countless of times in battle, his courage, mercy, and strategical battlefield thinking.

But most of all, all angels admired him for his unwavering love for God and the love and compassion he showed for his fellow angels even when some of the angels turned against Him. All angels loved him and had an immense respect and fear of him. Until one day, all that changed.

The second most powerful angel that God created, second only to Zamariel, was Baphomet. He is called many other names on different worlds. On earth, he is called Lucifer.

Lucifer was almost as skilled and powerful as Zamariel. Some would say, they were evenly matched. Others will say that Zamariel, always the merciful, gave Lucifer too many chances to escape his punishment for what Lucifer has done repeatedly over the millennia countlessly spreading vile evil and terrible suffering among God's creatures.

The third angel of God is Gabriel. Gabriel, for a time, became God's first angel after both Zamariel and Baphomet left the presence of God. Gabriel, the third most powerful angel of God whose loyalty that is only matched by Zamariel is the most loving of all angels. Like the angel Michael, he is fiercely loyal to Zamariel. He is Zamariel's right hand angel. For every battle and for every mission that the angels participated in, Gabriel was always in the midst of their planning and execution.

The forth angel of God is Michael. The other angels say that he, only second to Zamariel, is the most feared angel. A soldier who have carried out both God's and Zamariel's orders with extreme zeal and fanaticism. As much as Zamariel is compassionate and merciful, Michael has shown no mercy for those who betrayed God and Zamariel. At times, he is more feared than God Himself for his perceived mercilessness. Always ready to do battle, but tempered by Zamariel's reasonableness and restraint, has kept Michael at bay many times.

Otherwise, Michael's temerity may have caused more destruction that even He or Zamariel wanted. And it is Michael who defeated Baphomet and forever banished him out of heaven, as He wished.

As you can probably tell, in the beginning, the first four angels were greatly loved by God, but that changed over time.

During the span of 1000 trillion earth years, God created the universe and like a gigantic puzzle, created the pieces. These pieces are worlds much like the human earth and other worlds that are far different. The one thing that they have in common is that they believe in God in His various forms.

Every world had its own religious beliefs. Some worlds are made up of good people and live in complete peace and harmony, where in other worlds, wars raged since their existence. God sent his angels to every part of the universe to oversee his creation. Contrary to earthly beliefs, angels are not guardians of humans, but rather, they are guardians of God's plan.

That plan became in jeopardy.

You see, before God finished creating the universe, Baphomet, the second angel of God, took 666,665 angels and left the presence of God.

Baphomet did not leave God because God loved him less or because he wanted God's power. No, he left God because he was jealous of Zamariel, the first angel of God. He wanted to destroy the goodness contained in Zamariel and turn God's love against Zamariel. For that, God banished Lucifer from his presence. That in itself was hell that Lucifer created for himself. In doing so, Lucifer unknowingly disrupted God's great plan.

Chapter 5 Adram and Abdiel

Aslin was riveted by this story.

"So, what has this got to do with me?" Aslin asked before she could continue. "What is your name and who are you?"

Aslin had so many more questions. At this point he couldn't decide if she was an escapee from an insane asylum or this was some sort of a trick.

"My name is Abdiel. I am an angel sent by God."

Aslin could not help it and he regretted as soon as he did, he chuckled out loud at this declaration. He did not want to embarrass her no matter how crazy he thought she was, so he quickly stopped giggling as his face turned red with somewhat amused smirk on his face.

And then, it dawned on him; she called him "Zamariel".

A sudden distant rumble could be heard outside.

As Aslin was about to prod her with his next question, the distant rumble heard a few seconds ago approached them like a freight train. In few seconds, the loud rumbling sound reached its crescendo so ear piercing that Aslin had to cover his ears with both hands.

As he looked up in pain at Abdiel, he had never

seen such fear on a person's face, angel or not. She grabbed his right arm and lifted him off of his feet like a rag doll. She ran with him flying through the air behind her. She stopped in the living room wildly looking around towards the ceiling and listening to the deafening silence that was left by the aftermath of the shrill crash that ended a second ago.

"They found us!" Abdiel shouted while looking upwards towards an unseen area of the ceiling that gave no hint of the source of her fear.

She let Aslin's hand go and stepped back. Her white gown grew brighter as she bowed her head and from her hands and eyes, streaks of bright light illuminated the entire room.

The intensity of the light forced Aslin's back against the wall. Abdiel's form grew almost twice her original size and before his eyes, as she arched her back, a loud cracking sound could be heard as her back opened in two places. From them, grew what look like white antlers. The antlers grew hair and then turned into flowing feathers to form wings like an eagle, but 10 times greater in its wingspan. The transformed Abdiel filled the entire living room. Still glowing in its intense brightness, stood Abdiel, an angel.

Before Aslin could process what he was seeing and what it meant, she grabbed him by the hand and like a child, he was whipped behind her as they both flew through the air. Right as Aslin looked up, her head smashed through the two-inch thick front door like tissue paper. He was sure that she would be bleeding from her head and knocked unconscious and him, as a result of the assault on the door, would be tumbling on the wet grassy knoll of the front yard. But to his utter surprise, instead of plummeting to the ground, they were cutting through the wind and rain with fierceness of speed that trees, cars and houses were blurring past them. The rain was shelling him like tiny rapid firing bullets against his bare face. Aslin looked down and noticed that Abdiel's feet were not touching the ground nor was his.

After few minutes of this breathtaking speed, Abdiel noticed that Aslin face was contorted in physical pain as his arm felt like it was being pulled out of its socket, so she stopped at a front of a house as she and Aslin landed like a fighter jet on an aircraft carrier.

As Abdiel let his hand go and since his rubbery legs couldn't hold his weight after that exhausting travel through the air, Aslin toppled on his back on someone's wet front lawn. He lay there on the moist grass thinking that this must be some sort of really weird dream that he was having and he will wake up soon.

The rain stopped. It was eerily quiet; no birds could be heard, nor grasshoppers playing their nightly symphonies. The moon slowly peered through the opening created by the parting rain clouds.

Whatever sound they heard back at the house did not follow them.

"No one is home. Let's go in and you can dry off."

Abdiel kept searching the skies with an expectant worry on her face. She was shaking. Her wings drooped towards the ground; its tips touching the grass.

Before they could take another step, they saw an intimidating looking brute of a man appear at the front door of the house. He was a giant; at least seven foot tall and magnificent. He was handsome and alluring. Aslin could see that he was wearing a dark two-piece suit except without a tie or an overcoat and was bare footed. Through his clothes, it revealed rippling biceps and legs so thick that it looked inhuman. Even from that distance, Aslin could see his eyes. It was red and beautiful.

"Adram!" Abdiel screeched breathlessly and with great fear in her eyes.

"Give him to us, Abdiel! He is one of us", said the brute between clench teeth.

"Never! Do not interfere with His command," Abdiel hoarsely replied.

From her right hand a flaming sword magically appeared. The blue handle was encrusted with tiny little white diamonds. On its blade, a carving with a symbol of "Oo" appeared.

In an instant, Abdiel transformed from a beautiful angel into a powerful armor laden soldier. Armor, in the color of snow, covered all parts of her body except her face. Her great wings rose over her head and compressed together into a tucked position; to be ready, not to fly, but to charge.

The brute just laughed. He laughed so hard, he bent over from his waist and laughed harder as he looked up to see the flaming sword.

"Do you...really...think...you can...protect him from me with...your powers," more laughter.

Aslin could see in Abdiel's eyes turn from fear to conviction. The same look that Aslin seen in the old folks home where Aslin volunteered to read to the dying grand pops and grand moms; the look of courage and conviction right before they pass. A blow of wind caught her hair away from her face and it revealed the same beautiful face, but this time, it showed not fear, but determination as she rushed towards the man called Adram.

Adram, seeing Abdiel's ferociousness of her charge towards him, matched Abdiel's fierceness with his own with a warrior's cry that pierced the darkness.

In the midst of Adram's rush towards Abdiel, he, too, transformed with an amazing speed into an angel. Wings as wide as Abdiel's but as black as hers were white and the armor to match.

Abdiel charged with both hands on the flaming sword. Out of nowhere, fiery sword appeared in the hands of Adram during his split second transformation and just as quickly, Adram appeared on the right side of Abdiel immediately halting her charge.

From behind, Aslin could see the flaming tip of Adram's sword protruding from Abdiel's back. As quick as the battle begun, it was over. As he withdrew the sword, a loud painful gasp came out of Abdiel's mouth before she fell softly to the ground.

"Adram, if you love Him, please, do no harm to Zamariel," she panted, "He is not ready."

Forsaking his own safety and perhaps still thinking that this was just a bad dream and no harm can really be done to him, Aslin rushed to Abdiel. As Aslin knelt down to examine her wound, he did not see any blood. Her eyes were translucent and Aslin knew she was dying.

"Protect yourself, Zamariel. You are the most precious and powerful among us. Others will follow. You must run!" It was the last words uttered by Abdiel.

At that moment, Adram lifted his sword and screamed, "You must be destroyed!"

As Aslin looked up, he could not tell if the sword was meant for Abdiel or for him or for both. As Aslin instinctively lifted his right arm up to protect himself against the blow, he fell backwards.

In an instant, as Aslin looked up, the full tilt of the Abdiel's sword was imbedded in the sternum of Adram's torso. A wide-eyed Abram dropped his sword and fell along side of Abdiel. Abdiel fell back and looked at Aslin and smiled. Her whole body became translucent and lifted into the sky. In a flash she was gone.

A loud scream came from Adram's mouth. His body soon too became translucent, but he arched his back while screaming with pain. He reached out to Aslin with begging eyes. Aslin did not know what to do, so he hesitantly reached for his hand. As he did so, Adram's eyes turned to an evil and desperate stare that immediately frightened him.

The pain came back with fierceness that made Adram make his final scream of anguish before his body lifted towards the sky and flew into the darkness.

Chapter 6 Battle Ready

"We need him now!" exclaimed Michael.

He unfurled his massive wings as he often does when is exasperated. This time, it was mixed with anger.

"No, he is not ready," softly replied Gabriel. "We must bring back his memory slowly or we will lose him forever."

Gabriel, the always the most reasoned and logical one, stared to his left thinking of the eons past where he faithfully served Him and Zamariel. The countless battles fought with hundreds of his fellow brother and sister angels forever perished by Baphomet and his minions. He longed for the time in the beginning when love and peace with Him alone was all that mattered. Now and forever, Gabriel believed, as long as Baphomet existed, there will be no peace in the multiple universes that He created.

"Why don't we just ask Him to bring him back to us now? It will be faster!"

"No, Michael, you know the reasons why He will not get involved. We must do it ourselves."

Ever since Baphomet betrayed Him and Zamariel, it seemed that He changed. In human terms, God became more reclusive. It seems He abdicated all decisions to Zamariel. Now without Zamariel around, Baphomet has the upper hand.

"We are losing the war. The time is short and they are getting stronger after each battle. The others will not fight with us without Zamariel." Michael implored.

Archangels Michael and Gabriel were in despair. Ever since God hid Zamariel, Baphomet has gotten stronger. Michael and Gabriel knew that they were not strong enough to match Baphomet's skill and cunning. And yet He refuses to get involved. The angels of God could only witness the evil carried out by Baphomet and felt powerless.

Baphomet and his legions perpetuated all of the evil throughout the millennium on various worlds. The atrocities committed from the earliest time of Man on earth were perpetuated by Baphomet's evil minions. Yes, living beings carried out the dirty deeds, but they were selected by Baphomet himself and given the opportunities to come into power to do evil. Some call it "luck" while others call it "being at the right place at the right time". These evil doers were at times picked by Baphomet as early as birth.

Only two angels were given the gift of soul sight. Zamariel and Baphomet had the ability of looking into the essence of someone's soul and ascertain their true goodness or in Baphomet's case, the skill to see the breadth of one's evilness. With this skill, on earth, he artfully directed carnages ranging from Roman emperors that slaughtered and abused countless victims in the most unimaginable ways to giving birth to the countless slave cultures spanning the times of ancient Egypt to the present sex slave operations. Hitler was but a minor triumph for Baphomet since it was said that Hitler was hidden for many years before he came to power and Baphomet himself groomed him.

Then, there are the other worlds. The massive civilization cleansing by Zenirs in the 9th universe. By far the worse cruelty inflicted by any world on its own citizens that by comparison what Hitler did seemed like child's play to Baphomet. It was his first true evil deed and truly his greatest work. A blueprint that Baphomet used to destroy other worlds throughout the millennium.

***

On Zenirs, life evolved over 185 billion years into a massive civilization.

The planet was roughly forty times the size of earth.

This enormous planet was a home to more than 120 billion Zenirians. Each ten billion lived in a city called Soraian. Each city was named based on its corresponding birth of its city of ten billion.

Soraian 1 was the first city, then came Soraian 2, and so on to Soraian 12. Each Soraian city was governed by a council of twelve. Each council elected one person to represent their city. The supreme Soraian council of 12 ruled Zenirs. The supreme Soraian council passed laws that governed each city. It was each city's responsibility to implement these laws and enforce them.

Zenirs was a classless society. Even the members on the council were thought of as equals to all others. Each citizen of the city when the age of 300 (equivalent to about 48 earth years) was reached, each Zen was eligible to serve on the council for twelve of their planet years. The life expectancy of a Zenir was about 500 years old.

Zenirs has two suns that rotate around Zenirs on the opposite side of each other. Zenirs has two sunrises and two sunsets. It takes both suns about 6.25 equivalent days to make a compete rotation around the planet. This equals one Zen day.

Their bodies were very similar to humans as it exists on the current day Earth. They had limbs of two arms and two legs. Their bodies were lean. Their sexual reproduction practices were similar to humans except sex was not advertised nor glorified. It was thought of an act of reproduction; no more, no less. They walked upright in a bipedal fashion much like humans.

The average height of males were about 7 foot tall while females were 8.5 feet tall. It has been hypothesized that males were smaller in stature because they took the physical burden of bearing babies, hence, the male body over time became less nourished due to sustaining the babies in the womb.

There face was remarkably similar to humans; same shape of the nose, mouth, and eyes. Since the gravitational pull of Zenirs, due to its massive planet, Zens, by comparison, were about seven times physically stronger than of humans.

Zens had one language called Omani. This language slowly died out, but still practiced by some, since over several billions years, they learned how to transmit their thoughts without speaking.

The early brain implants to assist them in thought transference evolved in to a permanent genetic trait adapted by the body. First there was resistance to this technology. The ability to block private thoughts were unimpeded until more research led to an advancement in technology that allowed one to control their thought transmissions out of their minds. Private thoughts remained private.

The homogeneity of Zenirians made it easier for their top medical researchers to find cures for diseases and prolonging life. So much so that Zens discovered a way to eradicate all known diseases and sickness that allowed them to have pain free lives.

Food was in abundance and healthy and artificially made. They ate only to sustain their bodies. Gluttony was severely looked down upon. Weather was controlled. Animals and all forms of vegetation were free to grow without any threat of consumption.

There was no starvation. No homelessness. No wars.

Zenirs technology had no rivals. Travel through space had no boundaries set by light or space or time. Instantaneous journey from one location on the planet to the next took less than two seconds.

Zenirs were united under one religion. They paid regular homage to one God. Through their religion, they believed that Zenirs was the first living planet that God made. They also believed that there are other living beings in the universe that God created. And someday God will allow His living creations to come in contact with each other. They believed in having a soul and an afterlife that consisted of heaven and hell. Where you go after your physical body dies is determined by God.

Zenirs was located in a universe that God first created. It was the first planet with life that God made. For over the last 5 billion years, Zenirs had no wars, no crime, no disease, no enemies, and no hate. Zens, from its ancient beginnings, practiced family unity and the value it brought to its community. Family life was valued above all others.

It was the perfect planet; a place that exemplified exactly what God meant it to be when he created his first world.

Until one day, a girl was born. Life on Zenirs forever changed.

Her name, Ptonx.

She was born of two Zenirians, Copol and Midir, who worked as technicians. Copol, the male was a doting father. Always nurturing, always understanding the ever curious child that was rapidly growing faster mentally then any of her peers. Midir, was the more logical and direct in her response to Ptonx's behavior. As a result, she took on the role of both disciplinarian and a teacher. Both loved Ptonx with all of their hearts.

Every Zen, starting at the age of 100 until death worked full-time in a job that supported the well-being of the planet. To keep life balanced and centered, each Zen worked one day for every seven days of rest.

Copol and Midir were one of over three million workers that worked in shifts to ensure that the flow of energy went uninterrupted to keep a size of a city of ten billion flowing all day and night.

Copol was one of 500 administrators at the massive power plant. Each administrator was assigned a power grid. A grid represented 20 million households. Each grid had a total of 6,000 technicians. Midir worked in the same grid as a technician. Zen technology brought efficiency and very low maintenance. Hence, the work at the plant and other jobs that Zens held to keep the planet sustained with energy, food, and climate was easy and non-challenging. Most of the time, it was boring.

Ptonx was a precocious child. She went through 15 volumes of cyclicals by the age of 25 which most Zenirians accomplished this when they reached the age of 95. At first, both Copol and Midir, were amused and delighted by this.

But then, one day, when Ptonx was 20, while visiting her parent's workplace, she figured out a way to shut down the entire power grid. Granted, it was only shut down for about 3 seconds, but it was something that everyone thought was nearly impossible to do. With all of the safeguards and the mindful eyes of over three million technicians that worked in the city, this feat by a mere 20 year old child scared some of the technicians. Soon the council of 12 found out about this and the news of this event spread through the entire planet. While council decided to keep an eye on her, some decided it was just a coincidence. And soon all was forgotten. Besides it was only for mere 3 seconds.

At age 62, she discovered that she was able to read minds. Zenirians communicated telepathically, but had the ability to close their minds like one would close their mouths when not speaking. But Ptonx found a way to burrow into an unsuspecting Zen's mind and read their most intimate thoughts. At first, the graphic images flooding into her head gave her headaches, but soon she was able to control the flow of thoughts by focusing on one person at a time.

By age 94, she was able to turn her ability to mind read into mind manipulation. One day, her companion, Axon, a boy of the same age, was teasingly challenging her of her ability to make others do what she wants as Ptonx claimed to him that she can do.

"I can really do it!" Ptonx shouted her thoughts to Axon.

"Yeah, right. Prove it!" He kept pestering her.

He outwardly smiled at her that looked more like a sarcastic smirk to her. This was beyond an insult to a Zen since outwardly insults rarely happened. Telepathic arguments have occurred among Zens, but a true insult would be to argue using physical facial expressions. So to shut him up, he made Axon bite his right index finger. Axon exclaimed in pain with his thoughts and fear in his eyes.

Strangely, Ptonx liked this sensation of causing someone pain, so she made Axon continue to bite his right index finger until his teeth crunched down to the bone. Axon's eyes went wild and his thoughts echoed in his head and made its way to his mouth at first as a gurgled from his throat to a muffled scream.

Shocked and surprised by the physical sound made by Axon, Ptonx quickly muted Axon's sounds by squeezing Axons throat with an imaginary hand using her mind manipulation all the while making Axon's teeth continue its fierce downward pressure on his finger as it severed it at the middle knuckle.

With the half of his finger in his mouth, he tried desperately to spit it out, but a force like a rod pushed it deeper and deeper into his mouth down to his throat. He gagged for breath. He lost color in his eyes as Zens do when they lack Ön, the air that Zens breathe. As he clawed his left hand in the air towards Ptonx, he could see the strange grin on Ptonx's face, full of amusement and satisfaction. It was to be Ptonx's first kill.

The sensation to control other Zens brought on an uncontrollable pleasure that Ptonx desire more than anything else. Every chance she got, she would practice her mind manipulations on anyone from Copol and Midir, her peers, and soon the council members. Through her control of her fellow Zens on Soraian 12, at the age of 119 (19 years old by earth's age comparison), she was treated like a rock star. Adoring fans who adored her, but did not know quite why.

By the age of 131, her ego grew larger. Her pleasure to control others knew no bounds.

To quench her thirst of her new found power, she took control of the council on Soraian 12. The other eleven Soraian councils on the planet after learning of this, demanded her resignation and reinstate the council on Soraian 12. She said she will do that only after all Soraian councils met with her to hear her case for a better Zenirian.

The eleven Soraian councils agreed and gathered in the great amphitheater of Soraian 12. As it is the case of all council meetings, it was televised, but this time it was not limited to one Soraian city. It was broadcast planet wide. Since it was known to many Zens that this was a conflict that has no precedence, almost all Zens watched the live feed.

"Thank you, my fellow Zens for meeting with me

today."

Before Ptonx could get her next words out, a council member, Thorian, from Soraian 9 stood up and asked, "Why have you destroyed millions of years of structure and order! We demand you reinstated Soraian 12 council and…"

Before he could get the next thoughts out, Thorian grasped his throat as blood spurted out of his mouth.

In shock with eyes bulging, Thorian glared towards Ptonx and with his right index finger accusingly pointed at Ptonx shouting with as much force he could from his little used vocal chords, gurgled out, "You, you, you!!!" as he fell to his death.

The council members sat in shock, then simultaneously shouted thought screams and accusations towards Ptonx. The anger that boiled deep inside Ptonx was a feeling Ptonx never felt before and she took pleasure in it.

She waved her right hand at the chaos in front of her and as quickly as it started, the shouting stopped.

"Let it be known that today is a historical moment in Zenirians history. We are entering the age of enlightenment and a new beginning. From this day forward, all Soraian councils are dissolved. I, Ptonx, of Soraian 12, am your Supreme Ruler of Zenirs. And no one will oppose me!" she proclaimed as she stood and scanned the room.

Further chaos erupted like a tidal wave of despair throughout the planet.

In the next 50 years, Ptonx cleansed all who opposed her. Cleansing, a term Ptonx fondly referred to, was a method of death by choking in one's own blood precipitated by Ptonx's mind manipulation of the throat. She became so skillful at this that she was able to kill hundreds of opposing Zens at a time. All Zens lived in fear.

At first, as a supreme ruler, she championed efficiency. So much efficiency that workers were no longer needed. Ptonx controlled everything in Zenirs from the climate to food production to even the power that her parents used to work on as technicians. She controlled all of this through her mind. Zens had nothing to do but to relax and find new ways to entertain themselves. Their entertainment turned to harmful self-destruction.

Drug usage to escape the boredom was rampant. Overdoses were common and expected. Soon, Zens turned to body mutilation as dullness of everyday life hastened through the entire planet.

Some Zens realized that their civilization was on a path to ruin and it was all perpetuated by Ptonx. Rebels against Ptonx was formed against her. They found a way to block her ability to control them. They plotted to kill her, but every attempt failed. Ptonx always discovered them before an actual attempt was even launched. The rebel numbers grew to the point that Ptonx decided to once and for all to annihilate them completely.

After a 25 year war, Ptonx's mind controlled army of ten billion killed twenty billion rebel Zens. But that was not enough for Ptonx. Soon she was able to grow her power to mind touch every Zen. She created paranoia in every Zens' minds and as a result they started killing their family members, friends, and coworkers. It spread like wild fire. Zens killing Zens. In one year's time, all 125 billion Zens died except for one. Ptonx.

At the age of 206, she was all alone and not able to touch anyone with her mind, she became a victim of her own dullness that she created. Realizing what she did, she grieved furiously. Not wanting to be alone, her powerful mind took over the rotational spin of the great planet Zenirs and hurdled it into their nearest sun forever erasing the existence of Zenirs and its people.

The first planet that God created was gone forever.

Angels have whispered that on that day, even God wept.

For this evil, it is said that the power possessed by Ptonx was given to her by Baphomet. And from that time on, all angels feared the evil in Baphomet and the destruction it can cause.

Chapter 7 Xathanael – The Twin

The door to the house was open. Aslin stumbled inside. He still could not believe what he just witnessed in the past thirty minutes. He somehow knew that his life is about to change forever.

It was a nondescript foyer. No furniture, no pictures. The foyer led to a living room.

"Hello, is anyone home?" No answer.

The living room held a green sofa with rounded padded arms and a black recliner with wrinkly worn out spots at the seat. Neither of them looked comfortable. Aslin was too exhausted to care. It was eerily silent in the house when he noticed that the rain had started again.

Abdiel said this house was empty and by all indications, it looked vacant. Aslin was exhausted by all the excitement. He just wanted to sleep, so not surprisingly, he wasn't hungry. Usually, in one sitting, he could eat enough food for three or four people. His mother always said that Aslin had a very high metabolism and it ran in the family. His mother and father didn't eat as much as Aslin did, but he knew that compared to what others ate in his high school cafeteria, their appetites were almost inhuman.

One time, Aslin had a friend over for dinner. The friend witnessed his parents and Aslin eat an amount equal to a week's worth of food that would have fed a family of four. A gallon of milk, five pieces of sirloin steak (thick cut, of course) with about two pounds of mashed potatoes with gravy, two large bowls of salad, and a whole pie for dessert and that was just for his mom. His father had a bigger appetite, so add another steak or three and another piece of whole pie. Since Aslin was the biggest eater, add to his dad's dinner intake with another three or four steaks along with his favorite, another two or three pounds of mashed potatoes with gravy. And don' forget, a pound of his favorite ice cream, French Vanilla! Aslin didn't know at the time that they were big eaters until he became aware of his friend's gaping mouth and stare of shock at them throughout the dinner.

To an outsider, they looked like desperate wolves keenly focused on eating their kill in silence. Afterwards, his friend in awe told Aslin that he never seen anyone eat as much food as they did without being 500 pounds overweight.

After Aslin told his parents about what his friend said, they realized their mistake. Their number one priority was never to bring attention to themselves. From that time on, he was discouraged by his parents from inviting anyone else for dinner.

Aslin walked over to the sofa and plopped down. He immediately fell asleep. He dreamt about his mom and dad. The happy times that they had. It made him smile in his sleep. A bright light woke him up as it pierced through his closed eyes and blinded him so much that it hurt his eyes as soon as he opened them.

It must be the morning sun, Aslin thought, and then he heard a whisper, "Shhh…quiet."

In front of him was a teenage boy about his age. He was dressed in blue jeans and a white t-shirt that said "Welcome Home" and the symbol "Z" imprinted on front of it.

Aslin had to rub his eyes because the boy standing in front of him looked vaguely familiar. Same color hair, same color eyes…was he looking in a mirror; was he still dreaming?

As if reading his mind, "No, you are not dreaming," said the boy. "My name is Xathanael. You can call me 'X'!"

With a smile, he walked over to the window and peered through the drapes.

Remembering the bizarre events that happened hours ago, Aslin asked, "Wait, are you an angel or something?"

If he is an angel, why is he looking through the window, Aslin thought?

"Yes, I am an angel. The sixth angel made by Him to be exact. And I am your twin."

"How can you be my twin when you are the sixth angel?" Asking the obvious and little annoyed with all this nonsense about angels.

He smiled, "You are as smart as I remembered

you."

He walked over to Aslin and stood so close to him, Aslin felt uncomfortable at first, then Xathanael grabbed Aslin by the shoulders and hugged him by wrapping his arms around his back and whispered, "Welcome back."

"I don't know who you think I am or who you are?"

"I am here to help you to remember and bring you back," Xathanael declared. "Bring you back to Him and to us and to prepare for the final battle with Lucifer."

As the disbelief crossed Aslin's face, Xathanael arched his back and transformed himself into an angel. He grabbed Aslin's hand and leaped into the air. In a blink of an eye, instead of the expected head smashing through the ceiling, they were flying through the air. Aslin could feel the warm heat of the sun on his back and the cold chill of the wind on his face as they were hurling through the open sky passing in and out of white billowy clouds.

"Where are you taking me?" Aslin shouted as he looked over to Xathanael.

Without a word and in a flash, they made what it seems like a sharp right hand turn in the air and landed on a rocky terrain.

"Where are we?" Aslin was breathless. He felt like

a rag doll while whipping in the air as they flew.

He peered over at Xathanael, who, in his estimation, towered above him at around eleven feet tall.

"A place where I will help you remember, Z."

"OK, enough with the alphabets. What do you want from me?" Aslin was exasperated and losing patience with all this mystery about him, of who he was and of who he is or might be.

At the same time, Aslin had to admit, he was in awe. It's not every day you get to fly through the air with some gigantic angel as your airplane.

"Z, you are an angel like me. Unlike me, you are the most powerful angel and God's second in command. It is time for you to come back and stand with us."

"Let me get this straight. You are an angel, Abdiel is…ah, was an angel, and I am an angel which I don't remember anything about. And we have a bone to pick with another angel named Baphomet or Lucifer or whatever his name is. OK, prove it!"

Aslin had to catch his breath. The incredible events was a bit overwhelming.

As soon as the words came out of his mouth, an excruciating pain that Aslin had never experienced in his life shot through his entire body. A rush of air came out of his lungs. His body shook so hard that it made his teeth hurt. Aslin shut his eyes hoping to force the pain from his head, but through the pain, Aslin heard cracking sounds like bones breaking. He fell to the ground on his hands and knees and then to his stomach as his arms and legs thrashed about in impossible ways. He could feel every cell of his body exploding in an orgasm of pain.

"Please make it stop!" Aslin implored at anyone that would listen.

Tears of pain dripped into a puddle underneath his head.

"I am sorry, Z. They told me that the first time will be very painful for you."

The pain lasted for less than a minute that seemed endless in its torture. Aslin got to his knees with sweat dripping from his forehead. He felt dizzy and nauseous, but at least the pain was gone. He struggled to his feet and soon noticed that instead of looking up at Xathanael, Aslin was actually slightly looking down on him. That was when Aslin realized that Xathanael was standing in front of him.

Aslin felt heaviness on his back, so he turned his head as far as he can to peer what was behind him. Aslin gasped in disbelief as great white wings unfurled from his back high over his head. Xathanael, too, looked with awe as Aslin stood straighter to balance himself against the weight of his newfound wings.

Aslin stood about 12 feet tall and had a wingspan of over 30 feet. Aslin was speechless as to the realization of who he was and of who he is. But still, he had no clue as to what role he has as God's first angel. That was about to change.

Chapter 8 the Orphan

Every Saturday, and sometimes after school on special occasions, Aslin can be found either of two places that his church sponsors. The first place is at the local retirement home called "The Guardian Manor" affectionately called the "Guardian" for short. It's a three story stone building that was built back in 1925. It houses 125 residents in a one bedroom suites. Some of the one bedroom suites are larger than others to accommodate couples.

The Guardian was once owned by a local merchant who did well during the prohibition in the 1920's. As a sort of contrition, as the legend goes, the rich merchant found God and donated his mansion to house the age and the homeless. Soon it evolved into a non-profit retirement home.

It is located at the edge of town. It sits on a corner of a treed lot that borders a city park. Right across the street sits a strip mall that has a Safeway grocery store as an anchor, a hair and nail salon, an ice cream store, Vietnamese Pho restaurant, a post office, and a county library. For those who are mobile, they can walk around the park at their leisure, shop for snacks, and browse in the library, or eat Pho.

The Guardian houses elderly people from the ages of about 70 to 100 years old. It is sad to say, but most of the people come here to die. Most have daughters and sons who have forgotten them. Others, like their brothers and sisters, if they have any, and their friends, have all passed away or were in similar situations spread out across the country.

Some have physical ailments like cancer, severe arthritis, or just simply have bodies that the years of long hard lives have taken its toll, while others suffer from mental capacity losses like dementia and Alzheimer's. The few lucky ones like Mr. and Mrs. Jones lead an active and healthy lives.

The staff at the Guardian are made up of Catholic nuns and lay people. The Guardian is managed by a nun. Her name is Sister Sora.

Sister Sora is an affectionate and a caring person. Both the staff and the residents love her. She lives in a tiny room located behind the main building.

Maybe because of her geographical closeness to the Guardian or because she simply loves to serve God and His people, she seems to be always working and always there to hold someone's hand or to listen to someone's sorrow and pain. She never took a vacation, worked long hours, and made herself available foremost to all of the people in her care. She is the major reason why the Guardian has been at its capacity for the past 12 years since the naming of her as the director of the Guardian.

Couple of years ago, newly elected young popular senator of 32 years of age, Cornelius Jones, reluctantly placed his parents there. He would have rather taken care of them himself. His mom and dad meant the world to him. Even with his busy schedule, he made time to call his mom and dad every day and to visit them daily when he was in town and not in Washington DC. He was so pleased with the Guardian and the way they cared for his parents and other residents, he made a point of meeting Sister Sora. He wanted to personally thank the person in charge and express his personal gratitude.

After his meeting with her, he felt like he met a saint whom he felt he was not worthy be in presence of. Sister Sora, as she does with all of her visitors, overwhelms them with her glow of a smile, sweetness, and an aura of pure goodness. After the meeting with Sister Sora, he contacted the local media to share his story of his parents and the wonderful care they were receiving at the Guardian.

The local news channel went to the manor and conducted a segment on the Guardian by interviewing Sister Sora, the staff, and the residents.

Of course, Mr. and Mrs. Jones gushed over the Guardian. When asked about their son, Cornelius, no one doubted what he meant to them. Both wept with pride and joy of their only child.

It was not a sort of attention that Sister Sora likes, but within a month from the interview, the Guardian became even more popular. Soon the waiting list extended from one year to three years. Calls from people asking how they can donate money flooded in. They had enough donations to expand the number of apartments to fill every new request. The three year waiting list came down to almost zero. It was chaos for about six months until things got back to normal. Thank heavens, Sister Sora thought.

In all cases, during his visits, Aslin feels like it is he who benefits the most. These "old folks", as the nurses would affectionately call them, were wise with experience and had tales that could make you cry or make you burst with laughter.

It is here also where Aslin met a special person. His name is Tommy.

Tommy just turned ten years old. He lives in an orphanage with other kids that number around 75.

The orphanage has children from all different age groups from infant to 17 years old. Like most of the kids at the orphanage, Tommy never knew his father or mother. The mother who gave him birth abandoned him on the footsteps of an orphanage, so he has lived there since he was about 10 days old.

The orphanage teaches their kids to be self-reliant as well as help others that are less fortunate. This is hard for Aslin to fathom since he thought that being an orphan should be counted as one of the less fortunate.

Tommy, in his infinitely optimistic outlook on life, viewed himself as the luckiest person in the world. And he was forever grateful in his little heart and mind for simply being alive and able to share is joy with the rest of people around him.

His always-smiling face and positive demeanor could put a smile across the grumpiest old codger.

This was not what made him special.

One time, an 86 year old man with emphysema and lung cancer, was strapped to a bed because he was throwing his bedpan filled with urine and feces at the nurses. The old man, Mr. Benjamin, was filled with anger and sadness. He had children who had not visited him in years and with no other living relatives or friends to speak of, was full of misery and pain. He had tubes coming in and out of every orifice of his body.

He was constantly sick from illnesses that varied from a urinary tract infection to pneumonia. Some speculated that his constant state of pain and illness drove him crazy. While strapped to his bed for his own protection and for the protection of others, he could be heard screaming throughout the entire floor.

"Oh my heavens! I wish he stop screaming just for two minutes!" nurse Jennie said with frustration.

Tommy, visiting that day, heard the screams too.

In the midst of the old man's hysterics, Tommy, quietly without being seen, walked into the old man's room and closed the door. In few minutes, the shouting stopped.

"Thank you, God, for the silence," said Doctor Alexia with a smile.

After about two minutes had passed, the head nurse, Nurse Jennie looked at the other two nurses and the doctor and asked with concern, "Wait a minute, should we should check on him to make sure he is OK?"

The three nurses and the doctor on duty looked at each other after what it seemed like a prolonged silence gone too long and could not be ignored any longer. No alarms went off indicating any type of distress from Mr. Benjamin. It felt odd to them.

After few more minutes passed, silently, as if in mutual agreement reached telepathically, started to walk simultaneously towards Mr. Benjamin's room.

Dr. Alexia slowly opened the door, trying to be cautious less she arouse Mr. Benjamin's hysteria again. The four curious hospital staff members peered into Mr. Benjamin's room without barely crossing the threshold to the room.

They found Tommy holding the old man's hand.

Tommy's head just reached over the mattress where his face was leveled with Mr. Benjamin's as he lied on his bed. The old man's arms were unstrapped. His head was turned towards Tommy. Tommy respectfully laid his baseball cap on the top of the dresser next to the bed.

The four witnesses stood there in silence as they strain to hear what was being said in the room. Almost immediately, they noticed that Tommy was softly crying. Nurse Jennie, out of fear for Tommy's safety started to move towards the bed when Doctor Alexia softly touched her arm and gestured for her to stay back.

They stood there silently watching and realizing that they were witnessing a miracle.

"I know your pain and your sadness, Mr. Benjamin. Let me take it from you and let us share them together," said Tommy tearfully to Mr. Benjamin.

Benjamin's eyes welled with moisture while forcing himself to keep his mouth from quivering. He could not help himself, but let out a sad whimper.

He openly wept at these kind words. No one in his lonely and painful life ever asked him to share his burden and grief. The four witnesses in unison silently started to weep at the kindness and the sincerity of the moment.

The four went back to their station as Tommy stayed for the next hour. Both old man and young boy talked about all manner related to the time where horses were the primary mode of transportation to watching movies on the iPhone and everything in between. It was a history lesson and an update on current affairs all through the eyes of an 86 year man and a 10 year old boy.

Nurse Jennie checked on them once to take Mr. Benjamin's vitals. She listened to their lively conversation and giggling as two boys sharing secrets and jokes that were only funny to them. As long as she has known Mr. Benjamin, she has never seen him crack a smile, let alone giggle like a child.

A miracle.

Before Tommy left the room, with the help from Nurse Carla, Mr. Benjamin's straps were taken off and removed from the room permanently.

Two hours after Tommy left, Benjamin called for Nurse Jennie. He gave Jennie a gold cross to give to Tommy on his next visit.

"I'm sure he will be back tomorrow. Why don't you give it to him yourself?" Jennie asked curiously.

Benjamin, looking out the window, replied, "I'm ready to go. Agatha is waiting for me."

Those were his last words. An hour later, he peacefully and with a smile on his face, passed to God's arms.

Tommy's gift is one of pure innocence of heart and mind and the ability to cross the boundary of pain into happiness. He is the example of what God intended. Unfortunately, somewhere in time, some of us have forgotten what it means to be God's children. Fortunately for Aslin, he had Tommy to remind him.

"And the angels who did not keep their positions of authority but abandoned their proper dwelling – these he has kept in darkness, bound with everlasting chains for judgment on the great Day."   Jude 1:6

Chapter 9 Lucifer

"Have you found him?" snarled Lucifer.

Sitting on a high back sapphire studded throne that glistened with sparkling red glow that surrounded the evil one, Lucifer ruled his domain like a king and treated his angels like a hated dictator.

"Yes and no," Malach replied warily, Lucifer's third in command. "Adram found him with Abdiel, but both were destroyed. Now we suspect that he is with Xathanael."

With contained fury, Lucifer unleashed a powerful ball of fire at Malach's head, but Malach expecting such an angry response and was ready, as such, ducked just in time as the fireball went over his head and hit a lesser angel behind him that was not as ready.

"If he is with Xathanael, then he is being prepared for his return," Lucifer could not contain the fear that momentarily flashed in his eyes.

He knew that with Zamariel's return, it would make it difficult for him to complete his plans. And by any means necessary, he must somehow destroy Zamariel. He has tried several times throughout the millennium to destroy him and with the last attempt, he came closest to destroying him forever. Now, that he is back he will have another chance and this time he will not fail.

In the last great battle, before God created Earth, Lucifer and his dark angels ambushed Zamariel.

Lucifer lured Zamariel to the darkest corner of the universe where God had left barren. On a dead planet as the meeting place, Lucifer promised Zamariel a truce in their many battles where thousands of angels have been destroyed.

Gabriel and Michael begged Zamariel not to go. And if he did go, they too will accompany him.

"Lucifer cannot be trusted. Every word he says should be thought of as lies!" Michael implored to Zamariel.

"Michael is right. It could be a trap. At least, let us go with you," Gabriel said.

"Michael, Gabriel, I must go alone. I do realize that there is a high chance that Lucifer is once again lying and this can be a trap. But, if there is but a slightest chance that Lucifer truly wants a truce, I cannot take the chance of breaking my promise of coming alone. If Lucifer can lay down his sword and come back to Him and to us, this will better help us to protect and fulfill His plan," said Zamariel as he unfolded his wings ready to take flight.

With that, Zamariel flew to his designated meeting place. As he approached, he could see why this planet was forsaken by God. A forceful defecating smell flooded up as Zamariel drew near the inner atmosphere. As he got closer to the rocky plateau of their snarled meeting spot, he could see Lucifer impatiently pacing back and forth between two large boulders. Zamariel gracefully landed in front of Lucifer with a smile.

"Ah, Zamariel, I was afraid that you will not meet with me, especially by yourself," Lucifer, with a sly grin as he looked skyward to confirm that Zamariel indeed was alone. However, Lucifer himself had with him his three most powerful angels standing behind him, Adram, Malach, and Chayot.

The three angels appeared from behind the left boulder and were in full armor. This should have alerted Zamariel to Lucifer's hidden motive, but Zamariel's optimism overpowered his objectivity.

"Yes, my brother, I am here to reunite us under Him. Come, let us embrace and fly together once again!" As soon as those words came out of Zamariel's mouth, Lucifer rushed into Zamariel's arms.

Zamariel thought that finally, my brother, Lucifer, can now return with love and forgiveness. As quickly as these thoughts came into his mind, it left and was replaced by another.

"It is not I who will rejoin with Him, but it is you who will join with us," whispered Lucifer in

Zamariel's ears.

Zamariel forcefully pulled back from Lucifer's tight embrace and looked confusingly at Lucifer's face as Lucifer pulled the unholy dagger that was buried deep in Zamariel's chest. Lucifer took joy at the trick he forced on the great Zamariel. Finally he has outsmarted the most cherished one of God.

Zamariel clutched at his chest. Surprised at Lucifer's treachery and disappointment once again at Lucifer's deceit, Zamariel's head bowed with great sorrow.

Lucifer's wicked smile turn into laughter as Zamariel's shape start to glow brighter. Lucifer could feel it. Finally, he has destroyed the great Zamariel. The joy and elation he felt of his trickery elated him!

"Join us or be destroyed!" Lucifer bellowed with laughter.

"You said you wanted to meet to end our battles and to call a truce," whispered Zamariel as he sunk to his one knee in pain.

"You have always been so naive and stupid, Zamariel! Answer me, will you join us?" Lucifer spitted his words into the air.

"You already know the answer. Please Lucifer, come back with me," pleaded Zamariel.

"Yes, I always knew what your answer would be. I

always knew you were weak. With every ounce of energy that I have, I will destroy you and His plan!"

Lucifer's three angels after witnessing their master's treachery, let out a collective approving grunt. In their full body armor, with their flaming swords in their hands, rose up high into the sky ready to launch against Zamariel.

"No, you do not have to do this, Lucifer. Adram, Malach, Chayot, stop! Come back with me! All will be forgiven."

Hearing these words from the most powerful angel, momentarily confused the three angels as they looked at each other with hesitation.

"You fools! Don't you see, he is only trying to trick you? Attack and destroy him!" shouted Lucifer.

As if snapped from a trance, Adram tucked his wings close to this body and like a missile, flew straight for Zamariel. As Adram quickly approached, his sword hung over his head ready to swing down on Zamariel's head.

Zamariel remain on his left knee with calmness that momentarily confused Adram. Right before Adram's sword was about the strike Zamariel's head, another sword appeared and blocked Adram's sword blow. The force of the block was so powerful, that it knocked the sword out of Adram's hands and it flew through the planet's atmosphere and into space. Defenseless, Adram retreated behind Lucifer.

The sword that blocked Adram's was in the hands of Zamariel. The shock and awe of the quickness and the ferocity of Zamariel's power temporarily halted the battle. Even Lucifer stood their amazed. Zamariel's deep wound inflicted by Lucifer slowly closed and left not a trace of a knife cut.

Finally, Lucifer gathered his senses, "Malach, Chayot, attack!"

Malach attacked from the front with a slicing parry to Zamariel's ribs. At the same time, Chayot attacked from behind with an upper thrust of his sword that was aimed toward Zamariel's right shoulder. Zamariel, anticipating both attacks, was ready with a counter move. What he was not expecting was an attack from above. Lucifer, at the very moment of his last command, flew high overhead and simultaneously, came down with his flaming sword on Zamariel's skull.

Zamariel was able to counter both Malach and Chayot's attack, but was not able to anticipate Lucifer's blow to his head. Lucifer's skull cracking assault knocked Zamariel unconscious.

As Zamariel lay on the cold ground, Lucifer stood over him with his flaming sword only few inches from Zamariel's face.

"Now, I will have victory at last! I am the greatest angel of all!" Lucifer screamed.

Blinded by treachery and ego, while the battle ensued, both Michael and Gabriel were hovering high up in the sky watching the battle unfold. To keep their promise to Zamariel, they did not interfere. With them, they brought 50,000 angels that were also hovering over the heads of Michael and Gabriel. When Zamariel went down from Lucifer's blow, Gabriel and the other angels wanted to attack, but Michael held him back.

"Wait, there is more than meets the eyes," said Michael to Gabriel and to the other angels. So they held back anxiously to see the next exchange.

Gabriel, with extreme apprehension in his eyes, could not hear Michael's words. He poised himself to rescue Zamariel.

Lucifer, with both hands, raised his fiery red sword high above his head ready to strike a final blow to Zamariel's head.

"Goodbye, Zamariel! He is not with you anymore!"

Lucifer's sword came down in an arc towards Zamariel's exposed head and in a split second before it reached its mark, Zamariel disappeared.

Lucifer's sword ripped into the ground like butter barely missing Zamariel's head. A rock, where the sword struck first, exploded under the crushing blow of Lucifer's mighty sword. Confused, Lucifer swirled around to find Zamariel standing behind him.

"Lucifer, my brother, I am sadden and disappointed. Again, you proven yourself as treacherous and deceitful. And once again, I ask you to come back to us and all will be forgiven."

"Never! Attack him and destroy him!" exclaimed Lucifer to Malach and Chayot.

But before they could move towards Zamariel, 50,000 angels and Michael and Gabriel flew down and stood behind Zamariel ready with their fiery swords.

Seeing this, Lucifer claimed, "Cowards, you have to outnumber us to defeat us! Next time and another place, I will destroy you, Zamariel!"

With that, Lucifer turned and unfurled his great black wings and with his angels flew back to where they came from.

"We should pursue him and destroy him once and for all!" exclaimed Gabriel and ready to command his 50,000 angels to pursue.

"No, at another time," whispered Zamariel.

"You don't think that Lucifer will ever change, do you?" huffed Michael with seething hatred and anger.

"One can only hope, my brothers," whispered Zamariel as he lifted towards God's home.

*Praise the Lord, you his angels, you mighty ones who do
his bidding, who obey his word.   Psalm 103:20*

Chapter 10 the Awakening

"How do you feel?" asked Xathanael.

"I feel strange, but at the same time I feel a sense
of…comfort."

Aslin, now Zamariel, did not have the words to
express his true feelings. He felt a familiarity with
his new "body", but felt awkward.

Sensing Zamariel's confusion, Xathanael took
Zamariel's hand, "This first lesson is to help you to
remember how to fly."

Before the last word came out of Xathanael's mouth,
both were high in the layer of the sky called the
stratosphere.

Zamariel felt light headed and dizzy from the
blinding speed that they flew the ten miles above
the earth's surface.

Aslin, the human side of Zamariel, felt
overwhelmed with the vastness of the earth's
surface. The majestic billowy clouds, as it laid miles
below their feet, stretched far more than the eyes
could see. Miles away, Zamariel could detect a
commercial airplane full of passengers. He didn't
know how, but he could hear the chatter of the
passengers inside the approaching plane.

Aslin took a deep breath and felt the thinness of the air. It made him cough several times. He instinctively knew that the lack of oxygen did not affect him. He realized that his initial physiological and emotional reaction to the bullet like ascension into the sky was a human one.

"What you are feeling now are human sensations since the human part of you still resides within you. So, like flying and using your other angel powers will affect your human sensations like the sense of balance, breathing, and eyesight." Zamariel looked over at Xathanael and realized that the words from Xathanael appeared in his mind without them spoken from X's mouth.

Aslin was confused and felt disoriented. He didn't know if he was going to vomit or faint.

Seeing this bewilderment in Zamariel's eyes and the slow growing paleness of his face, Xathanael transmitted another thought, "Angels can communicate telepathically. Michael said that in the beginning, you will have headaches and we should intermittently communicate via voice and telepathy."

This was too much to grasp at one time for Zamariel. His head started to spin. The clouds became a white blur.

Zamariel's head started to pound like a sledgehammer. His face turned green and his body finally came to the realization that he was not breathing. His wings that were once felt light, sagged under its weight like a ton of bricks, and to Xathanael's surprise, Zamariel began freefalling back to earth. Unconscious, as Zamariel tumbled head first then end over end, the feathers of his wings tearing itself from its roots through the clouds, Zamariel's wings retracted and became Aslin again.

A look of panic and dismay came over Xathanael. How could he not have predicted this? I will forever not be forgiven if I kill Aslin, Xathanael thought. Xathanael tucked his wings close to his body and like a missile-guided warhead, Xathanael dove after Aslin. Since Xathanael hesitated too long, he wasn't sure if he could catch up to Aslin's body and intercepted him before he reached ground level. Xathanael's mind was racing with the thoughts of picking up Aslin's mangled human body off the ground. As they reached the troposphere, the last layer of earth's atmosphere, Xathanael knew that there is no way he could reach Aslin in time.

"Hellllllpppppp!" Xathanael never screamed as loud as he was racing towards Aslin's falling body.

Seven seconds to impact. Six, five, four, three, out of nowhere, a great expansion of wings appeared next to Aslin's falling body. The wings did not flutter. The body that the wings were attached to move with Aslin's body towards the ground.

Two, one, two hands reached out and hugged the lifeless body and flew towards the same mountain that Aslin and Xathanael started on. As Gabriel laid him gently on the ground, a thick bed of grass grew under Aslin's body to replace the rocky surface.

Aslin slowly opened his eyes and as it came into focus, the familiarity of his surroundings became evident as he realized that he was staring at the ceiling of his bedroom. He slowly sat up with a remnant of an excruciating headache. With his two hands holding his head, he suddenly remembered the wings.

He bolted from his bed and ran to the bathroom mirror. He turned sideways and stretched his neck around as far as he could. What reflected back was his human form and as far as he could see there were no wings on his back.

He was almost sure that it was a dream. He cautiously walked to the front door and sure enough, it was unbroken and not smashed by Abdiel. Yes, it was a dream, Aslin thought, as he slowly turned back towards the bedroom.

"Zamariel."

Startled, Aslin quickly turned towards the front door as he heard his angel name.

No one was there.

"Aslin."

Zamariel quickly turned back around and directly in front of him stood Xathanael in his human form as the Aslin lookalike.

"So, it wasn't a dream," Aslin gasped with trepidation.

"No, Z, this is real," Xathanael gasped with a smile and this time his lips were moving as he talked.

Relieved and overjoyed that Gabriel came just in time to save Aslin, he could not help himself but to run over and hug Aslin tight enough that Aslin lost his breath. Remembering how fragile humans were, Zamariel quickly released Aslin from his grasp.

"I don't understand. I don't remember ever being an angel. I was born here. All my memories are related to me being Aslin and not as Zamariel," said Aslin while recovering his air and relieved that he was able to breathe again.

Seeing Aslin was distraught, Xathanael compassionately took his hands and led him to the living room sofa. As they sat knee to knee, Xathanael began the story of how Zamariel became Aslin.

Then God said, "Let us make mankind in our image, in our likeness, so that they may rule over the fish in the sea and the birds in the sky, over the livestock and all the wild animals,[a] and over all the creatures that move along the ground."   Genesis 1:26

Chapter 11 Zamariel to Aslin

There is a war raging between Baphomet, or better known on earth as Lucifer, and his demon angels and Zamariel and his angels.

As if to answer the puzzled look on Zamariel's face, yes, you and your angels, Xathanael began.

Before the universe was fully created, and before God's final design, Lucifer wanted all of God's creations to come under the angel's domain. That would mean angels would have full control over God's creations. This was not His intent. Like the angels, His creations in its various intelligent forms, were given free will. Unlike the angels, His creations were given freedom to choose and cultivate their own worlds, both good and bad.

It started with the first world that God created.

Zenirs was meant to be the blueprint for all of God's creations. Upon completion Zenirs, the angels celebrated with God. It was a joyous occasion for God as He wanted so. But Lucifer had other ideas.

Lucifer thought that these living beings were weak

and needed to be controlled. Lucifer first exploited Zenirs and tragically destroyed the first world. For that God condemned him and forever prohibited Lucifer from His presence. From then on, Lucifer went from one world to another, creating havoc and evil, always resulting in the destruction of each world he touched.

You, Zamariel was the first to realize what precious creatures He has created. These living beings were not created for our amusement, but as a part of His great plan that even you, I think, do not know its full importance. But you, with your unshakable faith in Him, disagreed with Lucifer.

Lucifer reacted with viciousness and went to Him and asked Him to destroy Zamariel and put him, Baphomet as the leader of angels. Of course, he was denied his demand, and it set the course for Baphomet's grand plan to destroy all of God's creations and the angels that were against him.

Baphomet began recruiting other angels that were of the same opinion of angel's dominance over His creations. Over the multiple millenniums, Baphomet and his angels throughout the universe have treacherously influenced His creations to do evil that ultimately destroyed whole worlds.

Your angels countered with the nurturing of goodness and kindness that is in every one of His creations. It's been a losing battle. We are losing more worlds to Lucifer and his angels from creations self-destruction.

The hate created by living beings proves to Lucifer that he is right in that all of His creation needed to be controlled since they are inherently evil and self-destructive. Ultimately, destroying themselves and what He has created.

As Lucifer's power grew, Lucifer became bolder and bolder. He spoke out against Him and you during the council of angels. Council of angels is a gathering of the council of ten angels that meet to govern the activities of other angels and their mission of carrying out His wishes.

It was at the last meeting Lucifer attended that he made the claim that he will destroy you and the council. After Lucifer destroyed the Archangels Jeremiel, Zadkiel, Raziel, Simiel, and Ridwan, the five council members, God decided to hide you from Lucifer.

He hid you, not because He was afraid that Lucifer will destroy you, but he was fearful that you would destroy Lucifer and his angels and what you will become.

You see, Zamariel, after Lucifer destroyed the five council members, you, the first of His Angels, the benevolent and faithful leader, became so enraged at Lucifer, you went chasing after him.

In your path to Lucifer, you destroyed 50,000 of Lucifer's angels with such vengeance and hatred, that He had no choice but to bury you in a human body, so that you can forget and come back eventually to your old self. You see, like humans, we have free will. If we don't control it, we can succumb to evil. So the plan was to place you temporally in a human body until your human body grew old and naturally past back to us as an angel after your human death.

But in the past 18 years, in your absence, Lucifer and his army have accelerated their evil deeds throughout the universe. Most of your angels, because you are not with them, have not counteracted effectively to stem the flow of evil perpetuated by Lucifer's army. At the same time, Lucifer knows that he cannot dominate all of what He has created with your presence in the universe, either in human or angel form. To convince the remaining angels to join him in his conquest, he must complete his mission of finding you and then destroying you.

After mulling over what he just been told, Zamariel hesitantly asked, "If what you tell me is true, then, my parents were not my real parents?"

Xathanael took a deep breath. He was told by Michael and Gabriel that Zamariel, from his human side, the part that was full of love and loyalty, will struggle with the separation of his human bond with his parents and the reality of who they really were. The best that Xathanael could do, they explained, was to be truthful and straightforward in his explanation, but expect the worse.

Michael and Gabriela, your human parents, are actually angels that volunteered to be your guardian while you were in your human form.

Angels, Xathanael explained, surrounded him throughout his life. Gabriel, the dog, their neighbors, and one time even their postman were all angels that had one common mission, to protect and guard Aslin's human form.

Unfortunately, in the span of 16 years of your life, starting from your conception, Baphomet and his army of spies came very close to finding out who you were. It resulted in Lucifer's soldiers raiding worlds and annihilating some of them, hence, in the battles that ensued, many of our brother and sister angels and both of your parents and Gabriel died in their earthly forms.

"So, they are alive?" Confused and slightly dizzy, Zamariel, now Aslin, went to the sofa and sat down with his head in his hands.

"Yes, as angels, they are all alive," replied Xathanael.

Aslin's mind felt so overloaded with conflict, he felt confused between his humanity and angelic form.

Finally, he asked, "How about Uriel? Was she an angel?"

"No, she is a human. And sad to say that since you have feelings for her, we had to move her to a safe place." While looking down at his feet, Xathanael was reluctant to share the next news, "I am afraid that Baphomet is after her and she is in grave danger."

"What?" Aslin could not believe that Lucifer would want to hurt a human, let alone someone as innocent and beautiful as Uriel. "Where is she now?"

"Running," as the word came out of Xathanael's mouth, Zamariel, in a blink of an eye, instantaneously transformed to the mightily angel that he was and soared into the sky.

Chapter 12 the Capture

It's Wednesday, the day of the week that Tommy always visited the old folk's home right after school.

As soon as the bell rang dismissing school, Tommy quickly said his "See Ya's!" to his many friends and hopped on his black second hand bike to ride to one of his favorite destinations, the Guardian.

As he pedaled the six blocks to his destination, he waved and said his various "Hello's" and "How are you's" to at least to 15 or so people of various ages and gender. Each of them, at one time or another, had the fortune to come in touch with Tommy and be forever fell in love with Tommy's charm and his pureness of innocence.

As he rode up to the front door, as always, was greeted by the director of the home, Sister Sora. She was 58 years old. She dedicated her life to God at the age of sixteen when she entered the convent. She was like a mother hen to all of the residents of her home and equally favored the staff for their dedication and commitment to serving all of the people who lived there. In the past year that Tommy has been volunteering here, he has quickly become her favorite person in her life as well as a favorite among the staff and the residents.

With her hands on her hips and her reading glasses slipping down her nose, Sister Sora, half shouted with glee, "Here you are, Thomas. We missed you!"

As Tommy got off his bike, Sister Sora walked towards him with outstretched arms as it was customary for them in the past nine months were so, to hug each other like they haven't seen each other in ages when it has only been since the last Sunday mass when the last hug also took place.

"I have a special assignment for you today, Thomas," she whispered to him less someone hear as Sister Sora led Tommy by the hand through the front door.

"Really? What is it?" Tommy anxiously asked.

He knew that this was a weekly ritual between Sister Sora and him. It was always a "special assignment" and the assignment was always a resident who was either a "hard case" or someone new who needed a warm welcome that only Tommy can provide.

Today, it was a combination of both. Someone new arrived on Monday and he was a very hard case. A hard case meant either the new resident was grumpy and very uncooperative which frequently entailed a lot of screaming and throwing. Or, it can mean someone who has completely shut down, doesn't speak, often doesn't eat, and just lies in bed listless and seemingly without hope.

There was never an in-between, it was always a screamer or a silencer, as Tommy like to label them.

"Well, we have a new resident that came in on Monday. His name is Mr. Bell," Sister Sora replied.

"Is he a screamer or a silencer?" asked Tommy.

"Definitely a silencer. He hasn't spoken or murmured a sound. You can barely hear him breathe. That's how quiet he is."

Sister Sora could never understand what makes people shut down like that. Even with her vast experience and education, it always puzzled her. But this one puzzled her even more.

Mr. Bell was not like the other "silencers". He felt different. He took his meds and took direction well, like sit there, move here, and take this pill and that. But, not only did he not ever speak, but he also never made direct eye contact.

Sister Sora with her PhD in psychology can give you a whole host of explanations as to what mental and psychological ills that Mr. Bell may be suffering from, but deep down, without knowing exactly what or how, she felt uneasy every time she was in his presence.

Because of this, Sister Sora, at first was reluctant to allow Tommy to interact with Mr. Bell. But what harm would come of him by just talking to him for ten minutes or so? Besides, Sister Carla, the floor nurse, will always be in the room, per the policy of having a staff member present at all times when an underage volunteer is present with a resident.

Besides, she saw first-hand some of the miracles Tommy performed with the hardest of residents.

The first time was when Tommy first came to her as a volunteer and it was his first assignment. He was able to tear down the thick hostile wall that Mrs. Kim had for years in just fifteen minutes of talking to her. Much to the surprise and shock of the entire staff and the most of the coherent residents, for the first time in anyone's memory, they heard Mrs. Kim laugh and then cry on the shoulders of a skinny nine year old boy all in the span of fifteen minutes.

When asked what they spoke about, Tommy replied, "We spoke about two things, one the birth of her only child, a daughter and how she used to love peanut butter and two, about how she lost her when she was only seven years old. She misses her greatly."

Sister Sora took Tommy to her office. "Thomas, just be careful. Mr. Bell is…er…seems a little…"

"Weird?" Tommy finished it for her before she could get the next word out.

Before Sister Sora could reply, Sister Carla walked in. As always her hair was made up in a bun and her clean white nurse's uniform was pressed with every crease and line in place with hardly any wrinkles. Hearing her come in, Tommy immediately stood up and turned to take the two short steps toward Sister Alexia and greeted her with a hug.

"Hi Sister Carla. Sister Sora told me you have a silencer."

With a broad grin on her face that turned solemn after realizing whom Tommy was referring to said, "Oh yes, he gives me the creeps…"

She was the type who spoke her mind; her mouth was faster than her brain.

"Sister Carla!" exclaimed Sister Sora.

She didn't like the staff expressing any negative sentiments or opinions about their residents, whether they are true or not.

"Please take Thomas to see Mr. Bell and take care that you provide proper supervision," commanded the resident director.

"Yes, Sister Sora. Come along Tommy."

Tommy waved goodbye to Sister Sora as he walked out of her office.

The Guardian has three stories. Sister Carla led Tommy by the hand to the stairs to walk up to the second floor.

"I will be in the room at all times, so if at any time you feel uncomfortable with Mr. Bell just say that you have to go to the bathroom and I will take you out of there before you can say another word. Okay?" said Sister Carla.

"Okay," replied Tommy cheerfully.

When they reached the top of the stairs, they turned left into a long hallway. This is the floor where most of the residents lived. Each resident had a one bedroom with a tiny living room and private bathroom. At the door of Mr. Bell's room,

Sister Carla tapped on the door, "Hello, Mr. Bell, can we come in?"

Without waiting for a reply, Sister Carla opened the door. Sitting by the window with his back door towards the door, was Mr. Bell in a wheelchair.

From what he can see, Mr. Bell had all white hair and wearing a flannelled colored pajamas. His head was resting on his chest either because he was staring down at his hands or because he fell asleep and did not give notice that he heard them come in.

Tommy let Sister Carla's hand go at the doorway and strode towards Mr. Bell. When he finally got there, he stood in front of Mr. Bell. To Sister Carla, still standing at the doorway, saw the back of Mr. Bell and the face of Tommy as he was talking to Mr. Bell.

Tommy, afraid that he may startle Mr. Bell, leaned slightly towards him and whispered, "Mr. Bell, my name is Tommy, I am happy to meet you."

Slowly, Mr. Bell raised his head. He had white eyebrows to match his white eyelashes that made his eyes appear redder than it really was. It gave him a sinister and evil look. This did not startle Tommy, but what Mr. Bell said, made Tommy's blood curl.

"I know who you are," a barely a whisper that only Tommy could hear, but a snarl in its undertone that made Tommy take a step back.

At that same moment, as Sister Carla saw the look of fear on Tommy' face, a look that she never saw before, took a cautious step towards them, her walkie-talkie she always kept clipped to her belt, suddenly came alive.

"Sister Carla, Mrs. Johnston went code blue. We need you!"

Code blue meant that the person was not breathing. Mrs. Johnston was right next door. There were sounds of running feet and anxious shouting for help from both residents and staff.

Sister Carla was torn between leaving Tommy alone and helping out with Mrs. Johnston. She was the only nurse on duty at that time of day.

"Tommy, why don't you go down to Sister Sora's office and I will come for you after this emergency."

"Sister Carla, we need you now!" This time the plea came from the hallway outside of Mr. Bell's room.

"Okay, Tommy, I will see you in Sister Sora's office."

With that, Sister Carla ran out in to the hallway and

the door slowly closed behind her.

That was the last time they saw Mr. Bell and Tommy.

Chapter 13 Uriel

For four years that seemed like four decades, she's been running from an unknown evil that lurked at every corner. Uriel felt like she was trapped and the only solace was remembrance of the love she had for Aslin.

It started shortly after her parents and she moved from the same town where Aslin lived. Oh how she missed Aslin. Call it first love; but it was real. She kept asking her parents why they had to move since they were so happy there. They kept avoiding her questions by saying that her father found a new job, but the truth is that after they moved south 1200 miles to Glendale, California, her father didn't work for almost a year before his tragic death.

They lived in a two bedroom apartment off of Acacia Ave. It was nice at first. A quiet multicultural neighborhood and close to the mall, but far away enough from downtown Los Angeles, that it seemed crimeless until the day that death came knocking at their second story apartment.

It was a night like any other summer night. Warm and muggy that forced the air conditioner to work overtime. Her parents were in bed and she in hers when Uriel heard a blood curling scream that she recognized as her mother's.

Uriel quickly rushed out of her twin sized bed. Without thinking, she violently opened her door so forcefully that the doorknob forced a hole in the receiving wall. She ran towards her parents' bedroom across the tiny living room that separated them.

She suddenly came to a stop at the bedroom door. The eerie silence came as quickly as the scream departed.

"Mom, Dad, are you OK?" Uriel called out while hesitantly knocking on the door and with her heart beating in her ear.

No response. The night air felt especially heavy at that moment; almost like breathing under water. Even the air conditioner that was running all day and night seemed to respect the moment by its own silence

"Mom?"

No sound.

Uriel rested her head on the door to listen for any hint of a sound, but none came. Before she could reach for the doorknob, the door flew open knocking her back with such force she flew across the living room and landed on her back. Luckily, the floor was carpeted, so the fall wasn't as hard as the sound it made as the door smacked her on her left side of her body.

She laid there what seemed like minutes in a daze. She craned her head up as she pushed with her elbows to see who opened the door so viciously.

Beyond the door frame, there was blackness. Fear turned to worry over her parents that forced her adrenaline pumping body to an upright position. She slowly stepped into the darkness of her parents' room.

"Mom, Dad," this time it came as a whisper.

At the doorway to the bedroom, she reached for the bedroom light switch located on the inside wall near the door. As she clicked it on, the overhead light cascaded down on a scene that can only be described as horrid.

Her poor unconscious father was pinned against the wall with his head resting on his chest, arms splayed out and his legs together with his right foot over the left much like Jesus on the cross. The difference was that his hands and feet didn't have nails in them. They had butter knives driven into the flesh of his palms and into the wall. His feet was kept together stuck to the wall. On the surface of the upper foot a top of a shiny metal shone. Uriel realized that it was the top part of the butter knife that was dug in so deeply into both feet, that it took the entire knife to embed itself through the feet and into the wall.

Uriel's speechless gaze of horror panned to the right of the bed where her mother sat in the corner next to the bed stand. Her head was between her legs. Her whole body was shaking, but no sound came from her. Uriel quickly rushed over to her and embraced her.

"What happened?" Uriel gasped with tears flowing from her eyes. She could no longer look at her father.

Uriel's mother, Sara, could only point to the empty wall next to the door. It was scrawled with dripping red letters; Uriel could only guess that it was in her father's blood.

It read: iT iS TiME

As Uriel mouthed the words, she looked over at her mother and asked, "What is that mean?"

Her mother could only respond with more sobbing.

Before Uriel could get the next word out, a bright light shone in the middle of the room near the ceiling opposite of where her father was hanging on the wall.

As quickly as the light came, it distinguished itself only to be replaced by the most beautiful lady that Uriel ever saw standing in front of them.

She had long flowing blond hair. Her face was so white that it look like a porcelain doll. She wore a light blue flowing gown. It was not like an evening gown. It was clothing much like what a nun would wear without the habit. But at the same time, the gown itself was secondary to the beauty of the figure in front of them. Beautiful, not like a model, but beauty that came from the inside.

"My name is Gabriela, your guardian angel. I was

sent by Zamariel. You know him as Aslin," proclaimed the lady in front of them as she laid out her hands with her palms up.

"And he opened the bottomless pit; and there arose a smoke out of the pit, as the smoke of a great furnace; and the sun and the air were darkened by reason of the smoke of the pit"   *Revelation 9:2*

Chapter 14 Hell

It is darker than any black color imaginable. The air, mostly odorless with a tinge of unrecognizable smell, only to be replaced by utter silence. The temperature was just cold enough to make it uncomfortable like getting out of a shower in the middle of a cold winter's night. The volume of emptiness is infinite. The fear it brings to the bravest of heart or the most psychotic of mind overwhelms any feelings of survival. It learns to adapt to the innermost fear of its resident and exploits it for eternity.

Torture of the flesh and mind are mere foreplay for its exquisite dismemberment of a person's senses. It picks and nibbles at the very recesses of one's fears culminating in a denouement of pure and unadulterated pain by the likes never imaginable and forever never to cease. This is hell.

And it is here that Tommy has arrived.

"Hello?" in very tiny voice, Tommy cautiously extended his arms reaching out for an inexistent wall.

Like a blind person, he crept slowly and carefully less he bumped into something. For minutes that seemed like hours, Tommy touched nothing but air.

"Hello," this time a little louder and firmer.

He stopped and allowed his arms to fall by his side. Where am I, he thought. How did I get here?

"Hello," the suddenness of the delayed reply startled Tommy.

As he turned toward the direction of the voice, a light splashed through the darkness from a source that he could not see, shining upon a woman that stood about twenty feet away.

She wore a long red one piece dress down to her ankles. The dress only exposed her hands, face, neck, and her red shoes. She had long black hair down to her lower back that was parted in the middle. Her eyes were black and unblinking. Her lips were red that was framed with a porcelain white face. Her fingers were long and wiry with nails painted in a fiery red color to match her lipstick.

"Hi," Tommy managed to smile, "My name is Tommy. Can you tell me where I am?"

"I know who you are," as she spoke these words, she slowly paced towards Tommy.

She was at least six foot tall, Tommy figured. Her long legs closed the gap between her and Tommy in mere seconds except Tommy didn't notice her legs moving.

"I gave birth to you," she stopped about three feet from Tommy.

Look of confusion came across Tommy's face. He never knew about his birth mother. No memories that he can cherish. Just a baby when he was left on the footsteps of the orphanage on that cold lonely night.

People at the orphanage that found him could not ever remember the cutest and most cheerful baby. Even in the bitter howling cold laying in the bassinet on the top stairs, they were greeted by a baby's laughter as they opened the door expecting another wayward mother looking for shelter for her newborn baby.

"You're my mom?" Tommy asked much louder than he intended.

"Yes, I am your mother. I am here to take you home."

Even more confused, he had so many questions about why he was abandoned, who is his father, why now, how about Mr. Bell?

"Home? Where is home?"

As if reading his mind, Tommy's mother knelt down to Tommy's eye level and said, "Sweetie, it's OK. I know you have many questions and I will answer all of them, but we must go now."

Tommy was reluctant to move from his spot.

Something deep inside him said to stay put, don't move from this location. She beckoned him again bending at her waist with outstretch arms.

He was so tempted. He never experienced a mother's love. Always dreamt of it. Fantasized that one day he will meet his mother and tell her how much he missed her even though he never met her.

"Well, can you answer my questions first?" Tommy hopefully looked directly into the lady's black eyes.

The lady's pupils that were of darker shade than her eyes, if that was possible, dilated and then shrunk to a size of a pin prick and then back to its normal size in a matter of two seconds. Startled, Tommy stepped a half a stride back. Tommy quickly realized that this was not his mother.

Impatient as always and used to always getting her way, she snarled.

"Why you little prick! You are coming with me, you little bastard!" she glared her evilness towards Tommy.

"Tsk tsk, Lilith, yee of no patience as usual." Out of nowhere, a man in a white suit stood before them.

He was taller by at least a foot than the lady named Lilith. Tommy felt so small and for the first time scared.

"Lilith, you are scaring the boy. You know he has to agree to come with you. You can't force him," he continued.

His eyes were as black as Lilith's. His face was triangular in shape. His nose was sharp and his lips were pencil thin. His hair was black and short and stood up from its roots. Except for his eyes, it was warm and inviting. He looked like any other man he seen on the streets busy going to work, waiting for the bus, hailing a taxi, and much like some of the loving fathers he seen with their sons at the park that Tommy always envied. The only difference was that he felt evil.

"Who are you? Where am I?" asked Tommy, confused and a little afraid.

Lilith and the man in the white suit looked at each other and started to bellow with laughter. Lilith was laughing so hard that tears were streaming down her face.

"I want to go home!" shouted Tommy, confused that they would laugh at him for a very sensible question and bit frustrated with his predicament.

Before Tommy could get the next words out, Lilith, in a blink of an eye, materialized in front of him. She wrapped her long slender fingers of her right hand around Tommy's throat.

"You little bastard! You are not going anywhere!"

She lifted Tommy of his feet and hurled him across the floor knocking him unconscious.

"Moses was looking after the flock of his father-in-law Jethro, the priest of Midian; he led it to the far side of the desert and came to Horeb, the mountain of God." Exodus 3:1

Chapter 15 the Gathering

On Mount Horeb, unseen by human eyes, 1,454 legions of angels gathered to witness the final transformation of the leader back to an angel.

Angels with majestic wings of various plumes and wing spans formed columns and rows as far as the eyes can see. In human terms, one would say it was an army. Soldiers carrying out the mission of God. Ready to take on any command and wish of the Creator.

Angels were God's first creation and His first love. For these reasons, they are infinitely committed to protecting what He has created.

All of the First, Second, and Third Triads of Angels were present.

There are nine orders of angels that surround God. These nine are further divided into three triads. Each triad consists of three groups. Each group has specific duties.

The first triad of angels communicate directly with God, then they pass on their knowledge to the second triad, who then pass it on to the third triad.

Regardless of the triad, any angel can be tasked to pass messages to humans. Angels, in general, are not to take human form and appear before humans unless specifically ordered by God, Zamariel, or through his generals.

The First Triad, the Seraphim's, the Cherubim's, and the Thrones, were in the first group of angels.

The four Seraphim's duties are as messengers of God, can take on human form when necessary, and carry out any order given to them by Zamariel and his generals. They are angels of love, but are fierce in their loyalty to Him and will do anything to protect His domain. Baphomet was a Seraphim before he fell to evil.

Cherubim's duties was to keep the celestial records and hold the knowledge of God. It was a Cherubim who led Adam and Eve from the Garden of Eve after they were expelled.

The Thrones were responsible to carry out God's judgment. They form God's chariot.

The Second Triad, the Dominions, the Virtues, and the Powers were in the second group.

Dominions, were like company commanders of a military. They take orders from the Seraphim's and the Cherubim's.

Angel Zadkiel is the chief of this order. They ensure that other angels carried out their duties.

The Virtues carried out the miracles that were prayed for by mankind when God permits it. It is the two Virtues that accompanied Jesus when he ascended.

The Powers, are guardians between earth and heaven whose numbers were depleted, as many defected to Baphomet.

The Third Triad, The Principalities, the Archangels, and the Angels, were in the last group.

The Principalities were responsible for mankind, its nations and cities.

The Archangels are messengers of God and who are the front line against Baphomet and his legion. Even though Michael, Gabriel, and Raphael are archangels, over time, their position and rank rose to supersede the original designation as a Third Triad angel. Their courage and heroism was displayed during the Great Battle of Angels. The Angels are assigned to every human at birth. They are our guardian angels. A guardian angel can be assigned to multiple humans.

Over 5,000,000 angels were on their knees to pay homage to the greatest angel God has ever made. Regardless of which Triad they belong to or duty they were forever assigned, the primary duty of every angel was to serve God and protect His plan.

As many angels that exist, there are that many correspondingly unique combination of armor and swords. Swords, as the weapon of choice among all angels, are ornately decorated. The armor design and emblem is unique to the legion that the angels belong to and each sword that angels carry into battle are also unique to each angel, Triad, rank, and duty.

Angel Jophiel's legion has an armor shaped like a triangle with the top half curved in a semi-arc. On its front plate, two crosses intersected at the bottom with a red flaming sword in middle point towards the sky. Each angel in the legion carries a sword decorated with each battle they fought in. For each angel that they destroy, a red stone was fastened at the guard and for some, it was also fastened to the pommel of the sword. These red stones were not to show victory, but is a reminder of the sadness it brings when a brother or sister angel made by God is no longer with them. Each angel does not take pleasure in destroying a fellow angel. It is deeply grieved. But each of Zamariel's angels know that it is necessary to carry out His Plan.

As Zamariel stepped forward, the entire legion of angels bowed their heads out of respect.

Zamariel stood tall and stretched his wings to his its fullest extension and looked to his right and then slowly swiveled his head to the left scanning each angel one by one. Flashes of memory fleeted into his mind of similar meetings of this size. It was before the Great Battle with Baphomet and his angels.

"I am back!" He shouted.

An explosive wave of cheers of joy and happiness from each angel resounded across the world for what it seemed minutes, but in reality only lasted for about 30 seconds. It was a sound made by angels that only animals could hear.

Simultaneously, dogs howled, cats hissed, elephants blared their horns, horses rose up on their hind legs, tigers growled, birds sang, whales flew into the air. Zoos all over the world filled with sycophancy of animal sounds that startled spectators and zoo keepers alike.

It was an animal phenomenon that the world has never seen and the media immediately picked up this rare event and broadcasted everywhere on every TV channel. People with cell phones and camcorders recorded their own animals joining in the simultaneous chorus and posted the videos on social networking sites like Facebook and YouTube.

Non-stop media coverage of newscasters and talking heads were discussing conspiracies to sunspots as to the animals' seemingly synchronized responses to something utterly unknown. As it unexpectedly started, the entire animal kingdom went its normal way.

"Angels of God, hear me. As you know, I have been away. It is with great happiness to be with you again."

A cheer rose up like a tidal wave through the rows of angels as the last words spilled out of Zamariel's mouth.

"My happiness", continued Zamariel, "is mixed with sadness. Our brother, once lost, I am afraid has been lost to us forever."

Without uttering his name, every angel knew whom Zamariel was referring to. Baphomet has created chaos and havoc in many worlds. He and his dominion has caused pain and destruction even in the kingdom of God where angels presided. With heavy hearts, each angel remembered their own personal battles, the destruction of a fellow angel, and feeling of anger and sadness that seem to never go away.

"It is time to end the reign of evil," Zamariel's conflict was written on his face as his eyes followed his head as he viewed the vastness of the 5,000,000 angels.

"To battle!" exclaimed Zamariel.

As the cheers receded, Zamariel looked at Michael that stood beside him.

An overwhelming sadness came over Zamariel's face like a dark cloud. A look that Michael last seen many millennium years ago when God ordered Zamariel to expel Baphomet from the heavens for eternity.

"What is wrong, Zamariel?" Michael asked cautiously and with concern.

"He has Tommy." Without another word, in an instant before Michael could reply, Zamariel disappeared into the sky.

All of the angels knew instantly why Zamariel left abruptly. He telepathically transmitted their next mission.

When angels sinned, God did not spare them: he sent them down into the underworld and consigned them to the dark abyss to be held there until the Judgement. 2 Peter 2:4

Chapter 16 the Search

Zamariel is confused. He knows that Tommy is no longer on earth. He knows that he is with Baphomet, Lucifer. And he alone can save him.

But, even with his vast powers granted to him by God, he cannot seem to locate Tommy anywhere in the universe.

He calls his archangels to his side, Gabriel and Michael.

"Where has Lucifer taken Tommy?" he asks rhetorically.

Gabriel and Michael did not answer since they too had no idea.

In attempt to distract Zamariel's frustration and despair, Michael said, "Gabriela has found Uriel."

Zamariel turned and replied, "Uriel? The same girl…"

"Yes, Zamariel, she is alive, but in danger."

"Take me to her," with that Zamariel turned back

to Aslin.

In a blink of an eye, Zamariel, Michael, Gabriel, and now joined by Gabriela, appeared on the sidewalk in the front of the library located on Front Street in downtown Issaquah, Washington.

Besides Zamariel, who is now Aslin, stood Michael, a tall black 18 year old teenage boy dressed in jeans and a white hoodie without arms and Gabriel, a muscular 19 year old Asian boy with a tattoo of a long broad sword up his left arm wore cargo shorts with a t-shirt that said, "Heaven of Joy". And finally, Gabriela, a tall blond, a wispy of girl barely 17 that has a walk of a model and the looks of an actress dressed in tight jeans and a white shirt sleeve blouse, led the way.

The group didn't look like a gang, but a racially mixed bunch of kids with purposeful look that was dampened by their escort, a tall skinny blond that turn every men's heads from cars and bars as she strutted down the sidewalk on the busiest street in Issaquah.

They walk past row homes, neat and well kept, but years have not been kind to the deteriorating concrete steps that lead up to each set of homes.

When they reach the house nearest to the music store, Gabriela bounds the steps two at a time and knocks on the door.

Few seconds past before a tiny barely audible voice behind the door says, "Who is it?"

"It's me, Gabriela and few of my friends."

The door slowly opens that gradually shows the face of a smiling girl. Dressed in a t-shirt and jean shorts and her hair tied in a ponytail, she could be mistaken for a cover girl with a next door appeal.

Gabriela hugs the girl in greeting and then introduces Michael and Gabriel. As the last person approaches inside the doorway, Uriel gasps at the never forgotten love of her life.

"Aslin? Is that you?" Searching into his eyes, she knows that it is him.

She rushed past all three of them right into the arms of Aslin.

In between tiny sobs of happiness, "I thought I would never see you again, Aslin."

"I am here now, Uriel." Aslin's breath was taken away as his heart ached for her for he too, for these many years, was thinking and dreaming of her. He wondered, as an angel, can he have such earthly love for another person?

"Aslin, I have missed you so much. You were always on my mind and in my heart," said Uriel as if she was reading his mind.

With that, she broke down in weeping tears that broke Aslin's heart. The awkwardness of the moment, especially for the matter of fact Gabriel, the destroyer of evil angels, lightly coughed to interrupt the moment.

"Come let us talk in private later and catch up. But, first we must talk about Tommy," said Aslin with a smile and as he rubbed Uriel's back as reassurance as he did many years ago.

Uriel nodded and understood the gravity of their situation as Gabriela explained on the phone, so led them to the kitchen.

Gabriela stood behind the sitting Uriel at the kitchen table. Michael and Gabriel stood flanking Aslin sitting facing Uriel. Uriel told her story of the past four years of running and always living in fear and culminating in the death of her father.

Aslin knew that somehow there was a connection between Uriel plight and Tommy's disappearance.

Michael was the first to speak after Uriel's tale and addressing Aslin directly.

"Lucifer is somehow convinced that your love for Uriel and Tommy can be used against you."

Struck by the word "love" and her name in the same sentence, Uriel gazed into Aslin's eyes.

"What does he mean that Lucifer can use us against you?" Uriel asked.

"What Michael means is that Lucifer will kill you and Tommy if it helps to destroy Zamariel, eh, I mean Aslin," replied Gabriel.

Confused, Uriel once again looked at Aslin and haltingly asked, "What does all this have to do with you Aslin? I don't quite understand."

Aslin gave a quick hard glance at Michael and Gabriel that was caught with full meaning by his archangels. He turned his eyes towards Uriel.

"You are in grave danger, I am sad to say, because of me. Let me explain. Gabriela has been assigned to you to protect you. I…, we, are angels."

Uriel shook her head trying to wake up from this nightmare she was living. First, they have been viciously hunted for four years. Second, her father was brutally murdered and as a result, her mother has nearly gone insane, and now, these people around the table, even her beloved Aslin, all claimed to be angels. To top it off, she is being pursued by the devil himself. Her life was overwhelmingly in despair and now this?

Before the meeting with Uriel, Aslin, with Michael's help, uncovered a long hidden angel power, the power to telepathically transmit images to humans. Aslin was out of practice. Any longer than two minutes gave him powerful headaches.

But sensing Uriel's pain after all of these years of suffering, without hesitation, Aslin, got up and walked around the table to Uriel and bent down to one knee. Without a word, Aslin covered both of Uriel's hands with his. Uriel felt immediate calmness come over her, a feeling of a burden lifted from her now that she is back with Aslin. She let out a sigh as she pour herself into Aslin's loving gaze.

Aslin lovingly and carefully took her mind caressing her with his thoughts. It is known that when an angel with this gift when used for the first time on a human can cause both excruciating physical pain and mental anguish to the recipient. None of this happened since Aslin's awakening as an angel also awaken his most power strength, the gift of love and compassion.

Aslin opened his mind to Uriel as Uriel accepted his entrance to her innermost thoughts, Aslin, like watching a video, took her to the various places of his past from the beginning of his transformation. The meeting of Abdiel on that stormy night to the introduction of the life of Tommy and to finally uncovering the truth of who he really is, the First Angel of God.

Chapter 17 Tommy

Lucifer is exasperated and in the least not amused by this little human child named Tommy.

He has looked into the deepest depths of human souls and has seen nothing but contemptuousness, selfishness, and depravity. Even the self-proclaimed righteous and the god-fearing demagogues have succumbed to the deliciousness of evil. No one in history has ever averted the temptations of sin. And that is why Tommy has become the most perplexing case.

As the second angel of God, like Zamariel, Lucifer had the gift to look deeply into the caverns of the soul and find their truest wants, needs, and the most treasured of all, their fears. No matter the turns and twists Lucifer has gone down, he could not find not even a single particle of fear or sin in Tommy's soul.

This could not be; not even the angels were this pure. Why the only other pure of heart and soul was Jesus!

Lucifer was beyond exasperation. His realization brought him to his knees and into tears. The tears were of joy that turned into a howling laughter.

Now, he finally has the weapon to destroy Zamariel and may be God himself. If he can turn young Tommy into his way of thinking or better, kill him and then possess his soul for eternity.

Either way, he will finally will win and rule God's entire domain.

But there is one complication. He cannot kill Tommy directly. Angels, as created by God, cannot kill any living being made by Him. Throughout history, disasters, wars, and calamities that have caused a great deal of suffering were perpetuated by Lucifer and his angels. They did this by influencing the dark side that resides in every living being. From the successful temptation of Adam on earth and the forbidden fruit of knowledge of God and bad to the greedy patriarchs on Zenirs that have consumed their world to disastrous ends, Lucifer and his dominions had their hands in them all.

So to directly kill a living being is strictly forbidden. Even if Lucifer wanted to kill Tommy, he would be powerless to do so. He must find a human to do his perfidious deed.

Chapter 18 the Secret

"It was recently discovered that Tommy is the genetic ancestor of Jesus," proclaimed Michael.

With this type of knowledge in the hands of Lucifer, and it must be assumed that he knows already, can cause horrific repercussions.

Michael, Gabriel, and Gabriela looked at each other with confusion and surprise. Before Michael proceeded ahead with his next anticipated comment, they knew that only one among them knew the answer.

"Tommy must be a part of His great plan, but we do not know what part of the plan he is part of. We can only guess that he is crucial to it. The only one that knows the entire plan is Zamariel." All heads swiveled towards Aslin.

Aslin stood. Concern with written on his face. He looked at each of them as if to acknowledge their presence before he declared, "My friends, I am afraid you are wrong. I do not know what plan He has for Tommy. I did not even know that Tommy was related to Jesus until Michael mentioned it just now."

The three archangels murmured amongst themselves, as Uriel gently touched Aslin's arm, "Aslin, if you didn't know about Tommy, maybe that means that the future has not been written."

All conversation stopped for if what Uriel said was true then even God would not know what the future held. That is not possible.

It is known that with free will, paths can vary based on choices made freely, however, in God's infinite wisdom, choices can be infallibly predicted only by God. But it is also known that since God can predict the future perfectly, He can also shape the future to fit his overall plan, a plan that He only knows. However, if God can't predict the future, it will have devastating consequences.

The one that can shape the future can have vast control over God's domain. How is that possible?

Lucifer knows this as well. With the future unpredictable, chaos will rein and Lucifer will have the upper hand.

Tommy is critical to the plan. That is known. What is not known is the impact Lucifer will have with Tommy in his grasp and his ability to use him for his evil gains.

"Be on your guard! If your brother sins, rebuke him; and if he repents, forgive him." Luke 7:3

Chapter 19 Saving Tommy

"Justin, honey, I need for you to do something for me," purred Lilith.

Justin, as his predecessors have done over the millennium, became one of the many lovers that Lilith has seduced.

Lilith, the sexy and alluring counterpart to Lucifer, was made irresistible to any living being both to females and males. All the while spinning her influence into the minds of her victims to do her will. Any resistance was negotiated in bed and Lilith was very practiced in the art of love making in all its forms in the universe. Like the most potent drug, one session of sexual contact with Lilith becomes an addiction that has no reprieve.

Tommy found himself back at the orphanage in his own bed. The clock on the wall read 6:00 a.m.

Was it all a dream? He could not remember how he got here. The last thing he remembered was standing in front of Mr. Bell.

"We found Tommy. He is back at the orphanage," said Gabriel.

"That's very strange. Why would Baphomet let him go," Michael with grave concern looked over at Aslin.

Aslin shook his head, "I must go to him and protect him."

"No, Aslin, that might be a part of Lucifer's plan to draw you out," Michael stated.

"There is no way for us to protect Tommy without going unnoticed. It's hopeless," proclaimed Gabriel.

Angels can roam undetected throughout the universe disguised as one of the indigenous. However, the disguise does not work with other angels. Angels can immediately see through any disguise.

"I can be with him," Uriel said.

"No, you are in danger already," replied Aslin. "Lucifer is looking for you too."

"Aslin, based on what we know, Tommy's is far more valuable than me. I can always warn you of any impending danger. Besides, angels can't kill us. At least Tommy will have me beside him at all times. Gabriela, can you watch over me without being seen?"

"Well, yes, I can, but if there is an immediate danger, I am not to interfere in the free will of a human being," Gabriela replied.

What Gabriela just said brought a new meaning to the possible plan of Lucifer's.

"That's it! You're right Gabriela. Lucifer is planning

to kill Tommy through the hands of another human being," Michael gasped as realization settled in like a hammer into a nail.

"If that is true, than the decision is already made," Gabriel looked at Aslin for a response.

Slowly, Aslin put his hands on Uriel's shoulders and asked, "Are you sure? It will be very dangerous and I..., we, may not be able to protect you."

Tommy on his bike pedaled to the Guardian. It wasn't his day to visit, but he had to find out about Mr. Bell.

Half way there, between his hellos, he almost ran over a pretty lady that appeared out of nowhere right in front of him. He skidded to a stop to about a half-inch away from smashing into the lady.

"Oh, I'm sorry Miss. My fault," said Tommy.

"No worries, Tommy," replied Uriel.

Puzzled, Tommy asked, "How do you know my name?"

"Oh, sorry, my name is Uriel. I'm good friends with Aslin and he told me all about you."

Tommy was not in the habit of talking to strangers, as the orphanage repeatedly instructed him, but as soon as Uriel mentioned Aslin's name, his face lit up like a Christmas tree.

"How do you know Aslin? Where is he?"

"He used to be my neighbor. And he is fine."

"I miss him. I haven't seen him in a while. Please say hello to him for me."

Tommy started to push off on his pedal when Uriel stopped him, "Wait, umm, can I walk with you? I have a message from Aslin for you."

"Really? Well sure." Tommy got off his bike and started to walk beside Uriel with both of his hands still on the handlebars.

Every several yards or so, they had to pause their conversation as Tommy return greetings from passerby's on the sidewalk. To Uriel, she has never seen the likes of Tommy. It seemed that he knew everyone and based on the faces that he greeted, all genuinely adored him. And who can blame them.

Just in the few minutes of meeting Tommy, Uriel felt the goodness radiating from him. Just standing next to him brought a strange calmness to her heart and mind. It was a feeling she has not felt for the past four years. The only time she ever felt this way was with Aslin.

"So, what's the message from Aslin?"

"Well, he said that he misses you and he will be by the Guardian sometime today."

"Really? He will be there today?" Uriel nodded her

affirmation with a smile. Tommy was certainly infectious and very likable.

"Actually, he may be there now."

Uriel's plan was to get Tommy to the Guardian and keep him there as long as possible. It is there that they all agreed that Aslin could meet them since he is one of the regular visitors and it will arouse less suspicion from Lucifer.

"Wow, that's great, let's hurry!" Tommy started to walk a little faster. Uriel wanted to slow him down.

As there were about to pass an alley way, Uriel said, "Tommy, let's take a shortcut through the alley. It will save us some time."

Tommy never knew that there was a shortcut and he been going this route for the past nine months or so. Normally, he wouldn't follow a stranger anywhere, but since Uriel was Aslin's friend, he didn't give it a second thought. Besides, he gets to see his best friend, Aslin, sooner.

They turned into the alley, Tommy still steering his bike while walking and Uriel at his side.

Half way through the alley, Uriel turned to Tommy and pleaded, "I'm really sorry."

Her pleading voice made Tommy stop. Uriel's eyes welled up with tears.

Before Tommy could say anything in response,

Uriel's right hand disappeared into her jacket and just as swiftly drew out a six-inch flint knife.

Tommy's eyes widened as the awareness of the situation became apparent. Before he could turn to run, Uriel plunged the knife deeply into Tommy's chest where his heart was fighting to keep it beating.

The bike fell to the ground as Tommy's hands reached out to Uriel and his mouth could only form the word "why" before he started falling to the ground. Uriel caught him in her arms and slowly sat on the ground cradling Tommy's limp body.

A wail of sadness emanated deep within Uriel's soul as she cried out, "Forgive me, forgive me, forgive me!"

Tommy's left hand reached up to touch Uriel's teary cheek as if to say I forgive you and then took his last breath.

Chapter 20 the Rescue

Gabriela, looking from afar away from the peering eyes of Lucifer's spies, watching in horror as Uriel wept over Tommy. She could not believe what she just witnessed. She swept her wings about her and disappeared to announce the horrific news to Aslin.

Uriel cried uncontrollably as her tears flowed down her face creating wetness on Tommy's shirt. There was endless blood flowing from Tommy's chest creating a river down the alleyway. At the end of the bloody trail stood Justin. Rubbing his hands with glee at what he just witnessed will bring a tidy reward from Lilith and just thinking about her made his manhood rise in his pants.

He slowly approached Uriel who still had Tommy cradled in her arms. Her crying now down to a whimper looked up.

"Good! Matter of fact, excellent!" shouted Justin.

"OK, I have done what you wanted. Now free my mother!" spitted Uriel.

"Now, now, all in due time dear," before Justin could let out another word, a massive shadow covered them from above and just as it quickly appeared, the shadow gave way to a hulking angel towering above them.

The anger on his face was so gruesome, Justin slowly backed up in fear ready to run.

"Don't move!" scowled Zamariel, "Sit!"

Justin dropped like a stone on the ground, trembling and petrified, as he came to the realization as to who it was in front of him.

Zamariel, now transformed into Aslin, slowly moved towards Uriel and the lifeless body of Tommy.

"I am so sorry, Aslin," cried out Uriel, "I know that you will never forgive me, but I had to do it. They have my mother!"

With great sadness, Aslin bent down and took Tommy into his arms. As he turned, angels Gabriel, Michael, and Gabriela, appeared in front of him. Without a word, he handed Tommy into Michael's arms. The three angels and Tommy flew and disappeared in a blink of an eye.

With a heavy heart, he turned to Uriel, gazing into her eyes and said, "Goodbye, Uriel."

And he too transformed into an angel and disappeared.

Realizing what this meant, Uriel cried out, "No, don't leave me Aslin! Don't leave me, please!"

"He unleashed against them his hot anger, his wrath, indignation and hostility – a band of destroying angels."   Psalm 78:49

Chapter 21 the Revenge

Zamariel looked down on the limp body that once housed the soul of Tommy. He looked to each of the faces of Michael and Gabriel searching for an answer. Tears started to flow from what was once the proud and great leader of God's angels.

He could not understand why they could not find Tommy's soul. It has never occurred since God made the first humans that a soul after death was not greeted by an angel to accompany them to their new after life. In Tommy's case, soon after his human form died, none of the angels, including Zamariel saw Tommy's soul coming out of his body.

"Zamariel, you must ask Him what he has done with Tommy," implored Michael.

"I fear that Lucifer may have had a hand in this," sighed Gabriel.

There is an unwritten law that souls of a God's creation is never to be touched and are given free passage to God's presence where He alone will pass judgment. Never in the infinite passage of time has this unwritten law ever been violated. But why would anyone do this?

If Lucifer truly took Tommy's soul, he is more

powerful than any of them thought or he is fool hardy and will gain God's righteous wrath. But since no one ever violated this law, none of the angels really know what the consequences are. They just know that they can't tamper with God's creations, especially their souls; they essence of their being.

Zamariel wiped away his tears and turned to take flight. As he rose to the air, he shouted, "I will find him. Go now and make ready all of the angels for battle!"

Startled, before Michael and Gabriel could reply, Zamariel was long gone.

Chapter 22 the Descension

Driven by anger mixed with great sadness, Zamariel searched throughout all corners of God's universe. He visited every domain and places that even other angels did not know. Secret places that only God shared with him.

The last place that he chose to look, not because of fear, but because of his own refusal to believe that it can actually happen, he went to Baphomet, better known as Lucifer.

Zamariel could see Lucifer from afar standing in his dark chamber watching Zamariel come closer to him. It was obvious to Zamariel that Lucifer was waiting for him.

Lucifer shouted out a sarcastic greeting, "My brother, with what honor do I have for your visit!"

"What have you done with Tommy?" shouted Zamariel.

"What, no hugs and kisses," smiled Lucifer.

Zamariel inched closer to Lucifer; their noses almost touching.

"Give him back to me," Zamariel gritted between his teeth.

"Temper, temper, Zamariel. You know what happened the last time you lost your temper.

Besides, what makes you think I have this insignificant human boy?" Lucifer was beyond himself.

He could not help himself but giggle with excitement. He now has the power. He will make Zamariel grovel at his feet. He will be the king of all angels.

"I know you have him. Give him back to me," said Zamariel as calmly as he can.

"Wait, give him back to you? He is meaningless. Since when do we own human souls to give back?" Lucifer strutted back and forth.

He was feeling such pleasure at seeing Zamariel's pain.

"Let's just say that I do have this boy. What deal will you make me?" the grinning Lucifer clapped in joy knowing that he had Zamariel in the palm of his hands and so easy to manipulate.

With a sudden fury and before Lucifer could react, Zamariel slammed Lucifer with the back of his fist against the side of Lucifer's face and in a split second followed with a sword raised above his head ready to strike a fatal blow.

Lucifer in panic croaked, "Wait. If you destroy me you will never see Tommy!"

Zamariel's sword came racing down on top of Lucifer's skull and stopped at the first layer of skin on Lucifer's skull. In disgust, Zamariel backed away.

"Where is he?" hoarsely grunted Zamariel still heaving breathlessly.

It took all of his will power to stop his destruction of Lucifer.

With a bellow of laughter, Lucifer pushed himself up from the floor. Now I got you. I will make you pay for all of the shame and disgrace you have brought me, Lucifer thought.

"Ah, yes, I will give the boy to you, but you must agree to a deal," the last word out of his mouth was drawn out like a hissing wind that annoyed Zamariel.

"What deal?" Zamariel asked reluctantly.

He knew that any deal with Lucifer was not a good one.

"You step down as the leader of His angels and make me your successor." Finally, what he longed for will come true.

Zamariel's face of shock could not contain Lucifer's glee. Only thing Zamariel wanted to do his slam his sword down Lucifer's skull and squelch his stupid laughter.

Zamariel stood there, lost and defeated. What can he do? If he says no, then Tommy will be lost forever. If he says yes, what chaos and evil will Lucifer bring?

"Well, what is your answer," Lucifer snarled again with a smile on his face that did not disguise his evil intentions.

What can he do? Did he have a choice? God made the angels to be the protectors of his creation.

"Yes, I will do as you ask," reluctantly replied Zamariel.

Chapter 23 the Return

Cold. Dark. A sense of loss. Tommy felt trapped. The last thing he remembered was the sharp pain. He knew instinctively that he was dead. He heard Aslin's voice. Then nothing. Not darkness or even a tunnel of light like some people described in their near death experiences.

The worst sense was the feeling of intense loneliness.

He could not move. He could not feel his arms or legs. He could see nothingness, an indescribable landscape. His body is floating and not floating; his sense of inertia non-existent. How much time has pass? He started to panic. If I am truly dead, is the state that I am in now that lasts for eternity?

"God, where am I?" prayed Tommy. No answer, not that he expected it. He prayed every night for his parents and to one day to meet them. His prayers were never answered, but he never gave up praying until now. He started to cry, but he could not feel any tears on his cheeks.

With extreme despair, Tommy screamed, "Help me!"

At that moment an intense white light pierced through the nothingness and blinded him.

As he hurled another "Help me!" into the light, he felt a gentle hand on his shoulder and a familiar voice, "Tommy, wake up. You're having a bad dream."

Blocking the intensity of the light, a friendly face appeared above him. It was Aslin.

Chapter 24 Declaration of War

Zamariel had no choice.

He was immensely overjoyed to have Tommy back. But, to allow Lucifer to take over God's domain as the leader of all angels was too much. Lucifer would spread vile evil and tremendous suffering to all of God's creation. He could not let that happen even if it meant that he would renege on his word to the devil.

Then, there is Uriel. She got her mother back as promised by Lucifer for carrying out her deed.

Aslin already forgave her as Tommy did. But, in her infinite shame, continually refused to see Aslin. He knew that as a human and as an angel, he loved her and wanted desperately to get her back, but first she must be able to forgive herself. In that, Aslin felt powerless to help her.

Zamariel, God's first angel, called all the angel's in heaven to a place where they have met over the million millenniums. It is a place where important announcements, proclamations, and decisions are pronounced. Thousands of angels of various ranks and appearances flocked to this location. Whispers could be heard fueling the rumors about Zamariel and what his return meant.

As the last angel appeared, Zamariel instinctively appeared in front of them. Elevated above their heads so that all can see him in full view, Zamariel unfurled his great white wings to the chanting of his name over and over again until it reached an ear piercing crescendo. Zamariel reached his right hand above his head and then there came a total and utter silence.

Zamariel slowly swiveled his large head from left to right. It felt to every single angel that he was looking directly at them one by one and each one of them shivered at the thought of his power.

"I have gathered you here my fellow guardians of His plan to ask you to follow me on a path that you may disagree with," Zamariel began.

"We will follow you anywhere, Zamariel!" shouted a mid-level angel amount the crowd.

And then it began, the chanting of Zamariel's name. Again, Zamariel raised his right hand over his head and chanting quelled quickly.

"No, do not be hasty. Please think about what I am about to ask you and then, after much thought, decide if you wish to follow. Furthermore, if you do decide to venture another path, then do not fear, I will not fault you, so have courage in your decision," Zamariel proclaimed.

Michael and Gabriel, who were standing near Zamariel looked at each other with curiosity. Michael gave a "what's up" look. Gabriel shrugged his shoulders in turn.

"I have made a pact with Lucifer," said Zamariel. It

was so quiet, Zamariel wasn't sure if everyone heard him or did he speak the words just in his head without transmitting his thoughts?

Before he could make another pronouncement, Raphael, one of Michael's lieutenants shouted, "Why Zamariel? We promised in our last battle with Lucifer that we will never interfere with him."

True. The last battle with Lucifer and his army was costly. It nearly destroyed the universe and all of His creations. Many of the angels thought that even He became fearful of the consequences of the actions taken by the collective group of angels. But mostly, the angels on both sides came to realize that Lucifer was more powerful than anyone expected and his evil was so deeply rooted it even puzzled Zamariel as to where Lucifer's wickedness originated from.

"I know. But the balance of the universe is at stake and we must stop Lucifer or we will lose that balance forever. We must act now," declared Zamariel.

He let those words sink in and then proclaimed, "We must go to battle against Lucifer and his army."

A start of a hush murmur rose surging into a chaotic shouting amongst the thousands of angels. It quickly escalated into caustic disagreements. The last war was very costly for both sides. The memories still scarred many of the angels.

With a fury of a thousand atomic bomb, Zamariel's sword unleashed a cataclysmic power that only angels could survive. It brought all of the screaming and punching angels to an immediate stop.

"Again, without any repercussion and you have my word on it, if you disagree with this declaration of war, then you are free to go and stay neutral," affirmed the First Angel of God.

Hundreds of legions and their respective leaders looked to each other. It did not take long before all of them made their minds up. Some have promised to never go to war again against the other angels, demons or not. The others, no matter what, were fiercely loyal to Zamariel.

With that, almost three million angels slowly turned and departed. That left almost four million angels that will fight to their destruction.

"We are with you," Michael declared as he swung his arms across the horde of angels behind him.

Zamariel saddened and surprised by the angels that left, quickly recovered.

"Let's battle!" shouted Zamariel as he turned towards the home of Lucifer, God's greatest creation of evil.

Chapter 25 the Great Staff

The word of Zamariel and his army traveled fast to Lucifer's ear. The memories of the last great battle fought a million millennium years ago was still fresh in his mind. To the ones who have immortality, a million years seemed like a passing of just a few days.

Even for Lucifer, the war of the angels left its scars. The scars that led to nightmares. As powerful as he was, the cries of his brother and sister angels will forever remind him that destruction, in any form, is evil. Even for the great evil one, even the thoughts of battle with Zamariel brought a shudder and fear to his whole being. But this time, he will not lose. Zamariel, once for all, will beg for his mercy and at the end none will be given. So, let him come. He was ready.

It was in the great hall, that Baphomet sat high on his gilded throne waiting in anticipation for Zamariel. He could sense that massive horde approaching him and the radiant power emanating from Zamariel's body. How he hated with such vehemence that it filled him with such rage, his own powers sent out darkness that no nearby life could withstand its appalling foulness. His dark angels were dispatched throughout the universe to spread evil and destruction in the most painful way unimaginable while his most powerful angels were nearby ready to take on the first wave from Zamariel's soldiers.

Before Lucifer could get his next thought formed, in an instant, there stood before him the greatest angel of God. Tall muscular built frame carried the magnificent wings on a broad back with equally built powerful shoulders that carried a head with a long flowing hair that tumbled down pass his neck. In his right hand was the great encrusted sword that over a thousand millenniums have slayed scores of angels who have fallen from God's grace.

"Welcome, my brother!" Lucifer shouted sneeringly.

Lucifer was apprehensive and excited at the same time. The thought that the first angel came before him at the foot of his throne almost made him giggle out loud.

"What honor do I have of your presence?" Lucifer said with a wicked smile. The same smile he had when he whispered the evil counsel in Hitler's ear.

Looking around, more out of curiosity as to where Lucifer has fallen, the throne he was sitting in, Lucifer's angels lined on both sides staring at him with a mixture of contempt and awe, Zamariel swiveled his head back to Lucifer and compassionately declared like a parent to a child, "I cannot keep my promise."

Instead of the expected scorn, Lucifer laughed slapping his knee with a snarl.

"My dear Zamariel. I knew when you made the promise that it was a false one. You are a fool!"

Between tears of merriment, Lucifer spitted out his joy.

Puzzled, instead of the expected anger from Lucifer, such displays of merriment from Lucifer put Zamariel on guard. Such reaction only meant that Lucifer had a plan. And most, if not all of his plans, were always up to no good.

"Ah, the great angel is confused, I see. Well, let me explain. You see, I knew that you would never keep your promise, so I made sure I had some insurance against your deception and foolishness," said Lucifer.

"I know that you will never see the truth of what I have been telling you for a millennium. I will be the greatest of angels and you and the rest of your flock with do my bidding for eternity," proclaimed Lucifer.

Still confused, "This will never happen. I will not allow it," stammered Zamariel.

This time, Lucifer let out a short laughter with a finishing snort followed by a sly grin said, "I have the Staff."

Dumbfounded, a shudder of fear went through Zamariel's whole body.

"Where did you get it?", Zamariel shakenly asked while thinking of the immense power that the Staff possessed and evil that can be unleashed in the hands of Lucifer.

Even he did not know where it is was hidden. Only He knew.

The Staff of God was only known to the first four angels and just a rumor to the rest. It was made by God right after He finished the last pieces of the universe. Like a giant puzzle, each piece had a purpose in His plan. The Staff would only be used if the pieces of the puzzle did not fit according to His plan. Because each living being made by Him had free will, sometimes, the puzzle pieces took longer to align themselves to God's plan. But He knew, because of this weakness in his creation, some day, the pieces may never fit. In that case, the Staff would be used to destroy the entire universe and everything in it. It was like a giant bulldozer except there would be no ruins. It would be just gone. As it was in the beginning, from nothing came something and from something, all will be gone. Forever.

With Lucifer and his army steadily spreading evil in every corner of the universe, the puzzle pieces are not fitting together according to the plan. Evil temptations are far easier to succumb to then to do good deeds, it seems.

Whether or not, the timing is right, or whether or not, the pieces are fitting together, the angel that possesses the Staff can wreak havoc on the universe and bring its eventual destruction for eternity.

"You do not know the power the Staff possesses!" shouted Zamariel.

With a laughter that came from the bowels that held the entrails of Lucifer's hell, in an instant, a powerful force violently lifted Zamariel and hurled him through the walls of Lucifer's strong hold.

"Be gone!" shouted Lucifer wallowing in his triumphant. In his hand, Lucifer proudly and with awe shown on his face at the power it contained, held the Staff of God.

Zamariel and his legion were hurled back with such force, it instilled, for the first time, fear in all of the angels. No one has this type of power. Only God.

Chapter 26 the Keeper

Zamariel was stunned. Where did Lucifer find the Great Staff? He must go to Him and ask.

Zamariel made his way to the Great Hall of the Divine. Here, are only few have passed through the gates. Only the select few were allowed. It is said that Peter, the Blessed Virgin, and Abraham resided here. It is here, where God sits upon his throne watching over his creation.

Before he could pass over to the threshold of the Great Hall, an old human formed man stood by the entrance.

"Zamariel, why are you here?" the old man asked.

This was very puzzling to Zamariel. He has never seen this man nor has he ever been questioned as to his going and coming out of the Great Hall. As the first angel, he had free access to God's entire universe including the Great Hall.

"I am here to see Him. Who are you?"

"I am the Keeper of the Staff. You are here to ask how Baphomet came in to the possession of the staff. Are you not?"

"Yes, how could he have taken the staff?"

Zamariel knew that even he could not take the staff without God's permission. A permission he would never ask for nor would the other angels even dare to ask.

"I gave it to him," replied the old man, the Keeper of the Staff.

"Why!"

Stunned and incredulous as to why anyone would freely give up such a powerful instrument of God to such an evil being as Baphomet was beyond Zamariel's comprehension.

Seeing his confusion and astonishment, the Keeper explained.

"When God hid you from us, not even He foresaw Baphomet's cunning," the Keeper began.

We don't know how, but Baphomet found out that God hid you in a body of a human boy. Lucifer desperately searched for you throughout all the corners of God's creation. At the last stages of his search, he found the staff's location by accident.

God has given me the powers to hide the staff, but he never gave me the power to withstand the evil powers of Baphomet. You see, I am not an angel, but once a man.

My name is Nehemiah.

"Nehemiah, the cup bearer?" asked Zamariel.

Yes, I am he. I am the 125th Keeper of the Staff.

Let me explain. As God deems, He has assigned Keepers before the dawn of creation. The first Keeper was an angel. Since the time of creation, there has been 124 Keepers like myself. Only once have the staff left its place. Unfortunately, that burden is what I bear today.

Upon hearing this, Zamariel disbelievingly asked, "Surely, God can force the Great Staff back from Baphomet?"

"It is not His way. You know that," replied the old man.

Of course he knew that.

"Then, we are powerless. Baphomet will bring a new age of darkness everywhere!" exclaimed Zamariel as he slowly paced with his head down and wings drooping and dragging on the ground.

Defeated even before the war started, what can we do?

"Not to worry, Zamariel. Baphomet can use the Staff to his evil advantage, but he cannot use it to destroy angels in battle," the old man said.

Chapter 27 to War

"We must go to war!"

"No!' shouted Gabriel.

Gabriel, the fiercest warrior among his legions, who was always first to battle and the bravest of them all, surprised everyone with this proclamation.

"I will not disobey you, Zamariel. I will follow you to the end. I always have. But that evil dog has the Great Staff. He cannot be defeated," red faced either from shame or from anger, either way, Gabriel desperately wanted Zamariel to understand that this battle may be the last.

High casualties for both angels and humans could be unavoidable.

Michael, the archangel, torn between the loyalty he has for Zamariel and his own reasonableness, also felt conflict that left him speechless.

The silence was broken by Zamariel, almost in a heavy whisper, "I do agree with you, Gabriel. We will have heavy casualties on both sides. But, I ask of you to trust me this one last time."

With a deep sigh, Michael looked at Gabriel as if to say let's do this, "Zamariel, you have all of our trust. If you say we go, we go."

Zamariel nodded, then turned to Gabriel's happy and handsome youthful face that everyone knows.

"What, me miss a fight?" said Gabriel with broad smile.

Smiling back, Zamariel replied, "Good. Here is my plan and why we will win."

***

Tucked in the corner of God's creation, there was a place called the Oblitian, the forgotten universe. It is there that exists two billion planets and stars. Some were inhabited with the beginnings of life, the single organisms ready for the evolutionary flight into intelligent life as designed by God. The other worlds were a barren wasteland and will remain so until someday God's creatures will inhabit them for their own purposes.

The Oblitian, in its infant stages, was the place chosen for the battle because it was the only place left that did not have intelligent life. Even Baphomet knew that having an open battle to be witnessed by humans would be catastrophic.

Angels are not to be revealed unless directed by God. A veil of secrecy must be maintained. Even the evil one honors secrecy even though he has perpetuated evil in different forms.

Thousands of angels on both sides met on this battlefield of space.

Zamariel, with his vast army of stupendous winged angels with the their magnificent full body armor and their fiery swords, formed in multitude of rows at his back, looked over the vastness of space only to settle his eyes at what was in front of him in the near distance.

Lucifer's followers, once a possessor of faith in the creator that was unwavering, now has been transformed from beautiful angels to a monstrous and hideous beasts of evil. On the battlefield, as they ready to go to war with Zamariel's army that will pit their fellow brother and sister angels that they once loved, instantly transformed into demons of hatred, all with a vile hatred of God and everything created by God.

"It is today, my brothers and sisters, that we come together as one," proclaimed Lucifer to his minions, but hoping that Zamariel's angels will also hear his prophesy of what is to come.

"Today, we will unite all of our brothers and sisters!" simultaneous snarling and hissing of agreement that only demons can make filled the void in space. Repulsive sounds of demons that only fellow angels can hear.

"Zamariel, I will give you one more chance to surrender yourself to me!" Lucifer shouted.

Zamariel knew that this was all for show. He answered back to Lucifer with a steely silence.

"Z! Z! Z! Z!..." a rising tide of chanting roared

behind Zamariel.

Lucifer was beside himself with anger and jealousy. "Destroy the bastards!" screamed Lucifer.

Lucifer's legion of angels swiftly formed a V-column formation with Lucifer at the point. Like a guided missile, the path to destruction came towards Zamariel.

As preplanned, Zamariel's forces employed a countermeasure by forming a U-shaped formation to swallow the incoming onslaught of demons.

So powerful were both sides, one did not have an advantage over the others. Even Zamariel, as powerful as he was, could not destroy enough demons fast enough. Since angels did not physically tired, this went on for days without a pause.

Angels against demon angels, with their fiery swords swiftly tearing limbs came countless cries of pain and the eventual destruction of thousands of angels on the battlefield. At each angels end, hundreds of angels can be seen lifting up to its final destination of annihilation.

As he waged his own battle against the demon angels, Zamariel could hear the cries of destruction from all of the angels of God even Lucifer's demon angels. Tears freely flowed as his heart broke with agony and sorrow as his fellow brother and sister angels fell next to him in total oblivion.

Lucifer too was aware of the elimination of his angels, but it didn't cause sadness in him. Rather, in his calculating mind, he subtracted the destroyed angels from his ranks and quickly realized that with fewer angels, less evil can be perpetuated throughout God's creation.

As both Zamariel and Lucifer realized, the war against each other was fruitless. For Zamariel, he could not allow more destruction of his angels or even Lucifer's. For Lucifer, for his selfish reasons, he knew that the only way he could destroy Zamariel's power was to turn every living creature that God has created to evil and to do that, he needed more angels, not less.

For those reasons, both Zamariel and Lucifer called a truce.

Chapter 28 the Truce

As a part of the truce, the staff was returned to the Keeper of the Staff and put back into its rightful place, but this time the Staff of God rested in a place where it will be unknown to all, but only to be known to Zamariel and the Keeper.

Even Lucifer realized that the power of the staff was not his right to own. He, who has created chaos and evil throughout all of God's creation and who have countless of times defied and disobeyed God, still feared and loved Him like a child to his Father.

As he turned to leave the sacred place where the staff will rest, hopefully for eternity, Zamariel could not help to think with sadness of the many battles against Lucifer and his dominion and how costly they were. Thousands of angels were destroyed on both sides and countless worlds were counted as collateral damage.

Zamariel took full responsibility for the chaos and suffering inflicted on God's creation caused by the angels on both sides as they clashed on various battlegrounds through the millennium. Even sadder, he knew that the latest battle will not be the last.

One positive outcome came out from this latest battle of hatred. As a part of the truce, Lucifer agreed to free Tommy's soul, so that his soul can unite with his body and continue to travel its way to God. In return, Zamariel will not pursue his destruction of Lucifer and his minions.

Zamariel went to God. He explained to Him, through no fault of Tommy's and because of the interference of angels in his life, he should be given his life back and be allowed to continue his life as he would have if it wasn't for Lucifer meddling. His life, since his death was forced by an angel, should be given a second chance.

Zamariel, who has the favor of God, who can only dare to ask the next request, inquired about Uriel's condition.

"Lord, I beseech you with one another request. Uriel, by her hands committed murder, but she did it to protect her mother and she is remorseful and has repented. Please forgive her."

Murder is one of the most grievous sins that humans can commit. By destroying what God has built was an automatic entry into the abyss. Zamariel knew this.

God infinitely loved Zamariel above all others both angels and humans alike. So, God agreed with one condition.

God erased Tommy's memories of his encounters with Lucifer and his dominions. He also erased his experience with hell and his moment of death. He put Tommy back into the orphanage to live out the rest of his human life.

Chapter 29 God's Indifference

After the truce, God looked around the vastness of the universes He created.

He saw the destruction caused by Zamariel and Lucifer.

He heard the begging cries from the multitude of His various creations in every language that prayers were spoken from every religion that believed in a single ever-loving God all pleading for mercy and a better life.

Since the dawn of creation, He heard the prayers for relief from both natural and creation-made diseases and wars that have inflicted all of His creatures. And Lucifer, He knew, had a hand in almost all aspects of his creation's suffering.

He was aware of all this, yet He chose to do nothing.

Then on the first day of Truce, He rested.

"They reported to the angel of Yahweh as he stood among the myrtles, "We have been patrolling the world, and indeed the whole world is still and at peace." *Zechariah 1:11*

Epilogue: From Aslin's Diary

I am happy today.

Tommy and Uriel are with me and we are a family. I will look after them until their earthly bodies die.

Note to self: I will need Gabriel's and Michael's help to carry out His condition.

The End

About the Author

Tom Brown was raised as a Roman Catholic in Pennsylvania, he went to a Catholic elementary school and high school.

He believes that miracles happen every day. All you have to do is open your heart and look.

He also believes for every evil in the world, there is tenfold goodness. These are angels working hard on our behalf.

He is happily married for 18 years and he now lives in the Seattle, Washington area.

www.ingramcontent.com/pod-product-compliance
Lightning Source LLC
Chambersburg PA
CBHW022129170626
46808CB00002B/917